PS
3535
.019
M39
Roberts, Wal...
Adolphe

Mayor Harding of
New York

.019
M39

OCT '75   APR 1992

'98.   JUL

APR '85

KALAMAZOO VALLEY COMMUNITY COLLEGE
LEARNING RESOURCES CENTER
KALAMAZOO, MICHIGAN 49009

29418

PS
3535
.O19
M39

MAYOR HARDING OF NEW YORK

By

Walter Adolphe Roberts

[Stephen Endicott, pseud.]

AMS PRESS
NEW YORK

 KALAMAZOO VALLEY
COMMUNITY COLLEGE
LIBRARY

MAYOR
HARDING
OF NEW
YORK

A
NOVEL
BY

STEPHEN ENDICOTT

T H E   M O H A W K   P R E S S
NEW YORK
MCMXXXI

29418

Library of Congress Cataloging in Publication Data

Roberts, Walter Adolphe, 1886-1962.
  Mayor Harding of New York.

  I. Title.
PZ3.R54398May8   [PS3535.01793]   813'.5'2   73-18602
ISBN 0-404-11412-1   1974

Reprinted from the edition of 1931, New York
First AMS edition published in 1974
Manufactured in the United States of America

AMS PRESS INC.
NEW YORK, N.Y. 10003

To

The People of the City of New York

CONTENTS

A Note on the Author

STEPHEN ENDICOTT was born in San Francisco approximately thirty-five years ago, the son of an Irish ward politician who had grown up under the wing of Abe Ruef, one of the Golden Gate city's most notorious bosses. Stephen remembers, when he was a boy, what a tragedy it seemed in his home that Ruef and Mayor Schmitz should have gone down together in the exposé of political conditions that followed the San Franciso earthquake.

Endicott is not his father's name, but his mother's, which he uses in this case for a series of obvious reasons. The Endicott family name goes back on his mother's side to John Endicott, first Governor of the Massachusetts Bay Colony.

As he grew up, his father's fortunes improved sufficiently to move from "South of the Slot" to the booming section west of Van Ness Avenue. By the time Stephen was eighteen, and preparing for college or business, his father was boss of his district. The very month the World War broke out, Stephen gave up the college idea and went to work as a leg man on one of the San Francisco papers. But his close connection with ward intrigues switched him, by the time he was twenty, to writing politics for the paper.

His father, seeing in him a certain aptitude for what may euphoniously be termed "practical politics," tried to induct him into the ranks of party workers. But the lad found that his interest lay in writing about and observing politics, rather than being in and of the game.

So it went until the United States entered the war, and Stephen enlisted in an infantry regiment. He was sent to France almost at once, was three times wounded in the St. Mihiel and Meuse-Argonne drives, and spent six months after the Armistice recovering from shrapnel in the back. He was then only twenty-three, and at his own request was discharged from the Army in New York.

He was lucky in getting back to his old work on a newspaper. He started covering police courts, but was soon put on special big-time assignments for a morning paper now out of existence. His natural affinity for politics reasserted itself, and he came to learn how Tammany ruled New York. All this was well, but when the paper he worked for was sold and merged with another, he lost his job.

He had enough money to get married to a New York girl and return to San Francisco. He arrived in time to see his father and mother die within a week of each other, and his father's local political organization immediately go to pieces because of the rivalry of several feeble would-be leaders.

Stephen then did some more reporting, and took a flurry in his spare time at fiction writing. But despite his happiness with his wife, he was restless. The visiting publisher of an English language newspaper in Shanghai, China, offered him a job as city editor. He went, leaving Mrs. Endicott behind.

China turned exciting at once. The Nationalist uprising was on. Counter rebellions, rapine and murder were the order of the day. He got into many bloody adventures, was almost put to death by bandits up the Yang-Tse River, but escaped. His paper was suspended, and he had the mad idea to go to Pekin, now Peiping, the ancient capital, which was in the hands of the older régime. There he was imprisoned for six months, and on his release by Marshal Chang he went on to Harbin, that extraordinary polyglot city where the Government is nominally in the hands of the Chinese, but where the Russians actually rule and the Japanese maintain extra-territorial rights. The night life of Harbin is the most garish in the world. The public women there, says Stephen Endicott, are mostly members of the pre-Soviet ruling classes of Russia, and their best customers are *nouveau riche* Chinese. The social conditions in Harbin have completely broken down the ancient fiction of white supremacy in the Orient.

On his return to Shanghai, Stephen found a letter announcing the death from pneumonia of his young wife in San Francisco. Grief-stricken, he plunged into new adventures. He roamed over French Cochin China, Siam and the Dutch East Indies, then worked his way back through the Panama Canal and the West Indies to New York, where he has been since 1926.

Again came the call to politics, and while holding a desk job in the foreign department of a New York paper, he joined the Tammany Club of his Assembly District, of which he is still a member. Endicott says that it should be noted that he was graduated in Republican gang politics in San Francisco, since that party dominates the California city. In New York, he thought it the interesting thing to switch to the Democrats, because they run New York. He considers it so much waste of energy to belong to a minority party, if one proposes to play municipal politics.

He formed an acquaintanceship, which ripened into friendship, with an old politician, who had spent a brief period in one of the legal departments of the city administration. It was this man who told Endicott a great deal about the figures who dominated government in the past, and who gave him an insight into a new kind of practical politics.

The resulting novel dramatizes the history of Boss government in the metropolis. From the times of Tweed, who went to jail for his indiscretions, through the

tenancies of the Hall by later leaders, many colorful
incidents were obtainable to lend conviction to the tale.
But Endicott's chief object was to show what the future
may hold in the way of graft and chicanery if existing
methods are not reformed.

The Publishers

MAYOR HARDING OF NEW YORK

CHAPTER I

"Go Get the Mayor"

THE telephone on Dan Fitzhugh's desk rang.

"Hello?"

"Hello, Dan? Grody talking." The low, husky voice came with its customary caution. "Listen. What time do you go to lunch?"

"About twelve-thirty."

"Here's the point. It's important, and I gotta talk to you. You telephone me at twelve forty-five sharp. Not at my office. I'm in a booth now. The number is Lackawanna 10754. I'll be here, see? You call me from a booth. Got it?"

"Okay!" Dan hung up. He stared out into the street as he thought about Grody, head of a big private detective bureau, calling him. Nothing unusual in itself, except this trick phone call. The instrument tinkled busily again, and his chief, District Attorney Jessup of New York County, called him into his office. Dan put Grody out of his mind until, at twelve forty-five, he inserted a nickel in a telephone slot in a booth and rang Lackawanna 10754.

3

"Hello?" It was Grody. "This is Dan. What's on your mind?"

"Is your booth door shut? Talk low now, and get this the first time. Here's the lay. Colonel George Portis called me in on a hot piece of work. I know what he wants, but there's reasons why we can't tackle it, see?"

"What is it?"

"I'm not gonna give you all of it over the phone, but it means spilling a lot of inside dope on the city. What Portis wants, I told him, is an insider."

"He ought to be able to find somebody. Isn't he the head man on the People's Franchise Union?" Dan was checking up.

"Yeah. Now, listen. Meet me in half an hour on the corner of Canal and Broadway, that cigar store. Know it?"

"Yeah. Okay, Mike." They hung up.

Both got there five minutes early, and after greeting each other, entered a cab to take them down to Wall Street. In the cab Dan said:

"Before I go in there, tell me what this is all about." He leaned his big six-foot frame back against the seat and looked sideways at the private detective.

Grody looked at him the same way and talked in a low voice: "He wants dope on the Police Commissioner—Ollendorff—and a few other things."

"What's the matter with you birds doing it? You've done plenty other stuff like that."

Grody made a face. "This is outa our line. Hell, he wants real dirt,—political dirt—and the flatfeet on my payroll can't handle a job like that. I told the old boy that what he wants is a guy like you."

"I'm an Assistant D.A., guy. Do I look like an idiot?"

"That's just why you're the kinda guy he needs," Grody said quickly.

"Count me out, Mike," Dan told him. "Look, I have a good racket where I am. I'm in with the boys, and everything is roses. Why should I take chances?" Dan stared straight ahead, thinking.

Grody's husky voice dropped lower. "I heard you were gonna be on the Democratic ticket for the Legislature next elections, and that they've let you down."

Dan stiffened imperceptibly. "You hear things, don't you?" he murmured.

"That was a lousy trick, whoever pulled it," Grody said.

"I know who pulled it," Dan added. Grody kept a grin off his face. Then he went on, as softly: "Didn't you tell me once that Harding stuck a knife in your back over—what's her name?"

"Madeleine Dennis."

"I thought maybe you're the guy to handle this job for the Colonel."

Dan said slowly: "I might be interested."

Neither one spoke until the cab had landed them in

Wall Street, an elevator had lifted them to the floor containing Portis' offices, and a brisk secretary had shown them into a large, sunny, luxuriously furnished office. Behind a mahogany, glass-topped desk sat a venerable gentleman with thin white hair and deep blue eyes. He got up when Grody led Dan in.

Grody crossed the room, saying: "Colonel, here's your man, Mr. Fitzhugh."

The old financier's steady gaze swung to Dan, who smiled cautiously. "How do you do? Do sit down, gentlemen."

When they had formed a little circle around the desk, the private agency man went right into it: "Colonel Portis, this morning I told you you needed an inside man to give you the information you want. This is the man, and he says he might be interested."

The Colonel looked again at Dan.

Grody's voice, husky and unctuous, continued: "Suppose you tell him what's on your mind."

The old man, who was known to the millions as a monument of respectability, and whose philanthropies had earned the respect even of the yellow press, cleared his throat portentously.

"I had better begin from the beginning, Mr. Fitzhugh." The cadence of the voice was oratorical. "You see, I have never taken an active part in the politics which control our great city, until recently when a large number of us formed the People's Franchise

Union. I am chairman of that organization, as you doubtless know. We took it upon ourselves—with some justice, I think you will agree—to pass on to the public our matured opinions of different elective candidates. We hoped to influence the voters to cast their ballots for honest men, irrespective of parties. But somehow, I regret to say, our collective judgments have thus far failed to carry any weight. We have talked this over carefully, and have determined that we need to put teeth into the jaws of our attack on politics. We believe now that the opportunity has come to do so. That is why I called upon Mr. Grody to help me."

"When it comes to private detective work, Grody is the king pin," declared Dan impassively.

"But he informs me that his employees cannot penetrate to certain inner circles of the political world. I am perfectly willing to accept his statement at its face value, and to believe that you are the very man we have been seeking to help us."

The Assistant District Attorney said: "A lot depends, Colonel Portis, on just what you want in the way of information."

"Ah, of course! I am told that you are intimate with all the prominent men in our city Government today. And also that you have a very apt understanding of how, in a human way, that Government is run."

"I suppose so."

"Now—" the Colonel's eyes suddenly gleamed with

anger—"we have here in our city a disgraceful situation. A criminal has been arrested, a man palpably guilty of murder, and deliberately—deliberately, sir, I say—his trial is being unjustifiably postponed because of its political implications."

"Carmody, you mean?" Dan knew he did, of course.

"I mean Joe Carmody. Look at that matter in detail, sir. The gambler Rosenberg was killed on last Election Day."

"Shot November fifth, died the seventh," Dan interposed.

"Exactly. They find the overcoat of this Carmody in his hotel room, yet they do not immediately arrest such an obvious suspect. They wait until, for some reason, he gives himself up. I call that a piece of infernal chicanery!"

Grody cleared his throat. Dan sat still and listened. The Colonel went on: "This Carmody, sir, is incontestably guilty. But why is his trial postponed and postponed? It is outrageous. The papers have attacked the administration, yet nothing is done. Now—" and he raised a forefinger in the air—"the People's Franchise Union demands to know why the Police Commissioner and his Department have been so lax! We are out to obtain facts that can be used to drive the Commissioner from office."

Dan's face lost all expression. The Colonel continued: "It would perhaps be better for me to say that I—myself—intend to pay for the necessary detective work, or to buy information outright if it cannot be had in any other way. I am the instigator of the move to uncover the corruption which appears to center in the Police Department. I shall not involve the People's Franchise Union until I have material upon which I can ask our committees to take action. And what I want you to do, sir, is—get Police Commissioner Ollendorff."

The old gentleman maintained his upright pose, and stared at the two men. Grody sat and looked out of the window. Dan stared back at the Colonel. The tension broke slightly when Dan lit a cigarette. At length, easily, he asked:

"Apart from the fact that I know the inside of all this, what makes you think I'll do it?"

"I will pay you a hundred thousand dollars for information leading to the uncovering of the Police Commissioner!"

The lawyer sat rigidly. This was bigger than he had thought. But he said: "You know as well as I do that that is only one reason."

The Colonel's brow puckered. Grody broke in. "Mr. Fitzhugh means that maybe he has other reasons too."

Dan picked up: "The men you want me to turn on are the men who have treated me very well. I have a good job, and I expect to have it, maybe."

"But you will work for me?"

Dan shrugged. "If you knew what you really wanted, I might. You're not very clear on all this."

A look of triumph appeared on the private detective's face, while the Colonel leaned back to listen. Dan went on:

"You talk about the Police Commissioner being crooked as hell, and all that. He doesn't mean *that*," and he snapped his fingers. The Colonel's ears pricked up. "And about Carmody. You think he's guilty. He's not at all. Some other gun did Rosenberg in. We all know that. But why should the big shots want to nail a murderer who did away with one of the rottenest, lousiest crooks in the city, a skunk who double-crossed everybody?" Dan couldn't help enjoying the look of amazement on the simple old face of the head of the People's Franchise Union.

He went on, making up his mind as he went that this looked like a good thing. Besides, he had good reasons to want revenge on the men above him.

Grody had been perfectly right in the cab. About two years before Dan had been pretty much gone on one Madeleine Dennis. But Firenze, secretary to Mayor Harding, had introduced her to the executive at a party given by the Hall. They all knew she had been Dan's girl, but Harding took her right away from the Assistant District Attorney. Firenze had let a grin split his dark Italian face. Dan burned, but what could he do?

Then there was the incident of the nomination for a seat in the State Legislature. Harding had promised him that for the election this coming Fall. But when Judge Walters, boss of the Hall, had squelched Dan's

"GO GET THE MAYOR" 11

name in preference for one of his own boys, Harding
hadn't even put up a fight for the son of his old friend.
For it was true, too, that Dan Fitzhugh, Senior, had
nursed young Billy Harding, then State Senator, along
the political byways. Harding had been grateful, but
young Dan found him to have no guts. Harding didn't
know yet that Dan had learned of his rejection. But
Dan did know, and that was the second of his two
reasons. The third was one hundred thousand dollars.

This was running through his mind as he continued
to straighten out the Colonel. "Let's go back a little
way, to the time right after Rosenberg was shot. As you
say, they found Carmody's coat in the hotel room, and
that seemed to pin it on him. But everybody forgot, for
a while, that Carmody and Rosenberg had identical
coats. Carmody had liked Al's benny, and had had one
made like it. When he left that room in a hurry, he just
picked up the wrong one. Now, he left it around his own
apartment where the Police found it, knowing that
sooner or later they'd get on to the facts about the two
coats, and if he destroyed it that would make him look
guilty. Anyway, he surrendered to the Police, and he's
sitting in the Tombs, for murder, without bail. Then
what happened? You heard that Crandall was going to
resign as Police Commissioner as soon as they returned
indictments against Carmody. He denied it publicly,
but then Harding came out, saying that Crandall would
be out, whether he resigned or was removed. But why

do you think Harding turned that way against his old law partner? He and Crandall were friends all their lives."

The Colonel was listening carefully, a baffled look coming on his face. Dan talked on smoothly:

"Well, here's the point. They put Crandall in there to take orders, pinch enough people to make it look all right. But a big case came and he botched it up. So Walters made up his mind Crandall was going. He and Tully—who'll probably be next Hall leader, by the way—decided that. So they made Harding turn against his pal. It broke the old bozo's heart. Then they picked on Ollendorff, a big, loud noise. But before that, Harding and Crandall, and later the Big Noise, got together and figured there was no use trying to get the bird who did in Rosenberg, even if they knew who he was. Besides, as I figure it, all of them on the inside owed Rosenberg dough and they were glad to get rid of him. Do you follow it?"

The old gentleman nodded slowly. "This is horrible," he said.

Grody threw in: "I told you this was your man."

Suddenly the Colonel sat up straight, excited. "Why, it just strikes me, Mr. Fitzhugh! What you have told me is enough to blow up the city!"

Dan shook his head. The man's ability to misunderstand was marvelous. "You can't prove any of that before an inquiry. I happen to know that's the way it was, but I couldn't prove it. The point I'm getting at is that Ollendorff, and Crandall before him, had orders not to find the guy who bumped Rosenberg. They only want to know where he is, but they feel grateful to him. The only thing they're really worried about is the list they knew Rosenberg had."

"What happened to it? I have read of the famous missing papers."

"They knew the gambler kept a list of people who borrowed from him, including Mayor Harding and a lot of others, and also of those he supplied dope to. Those were Park Avenue people, but they don't care about them. Anyway, when Brand—Federal D.A.— opened the safe, the list wasn't there."

The Colonel rubbed his hands together in a sort of stealthy agony. He was honestly horrified, disgusted.

Dan continued: "A lot of this is fairly common knowledge on the inside—and a lot isn't. Of course, what I say here is confidential. You can't prove a lot of it, but it'll give you an idea."

"Then—then—Crandall, Ollendorff, Brand, all these high officials, are only crooked tools?"

Dan suppressed a grin. "Brand is honest, perhaps. Anyway, he's in the other camp. He's Republican. He doesn't figure in this. The city is run, Colonel, by about five men, headed by Judge Walters. But he isn't going to last long. Honest Tom Tully, as I figure it, will step over him. Now I'll tell you how I think this Rosenberg business is going to turn out.

"They'll have the trial sooner or later and Carmody

will be acquitted. Why shouldn't he be? He didn't do it. The papers will squawk about the trial, and the board will let Jessup—that's my boss—be the goat. He's slated to go, and they'll blame him for anything that went wrong in the prosecution. See it?"

Nobody said anything, until Dan added softly: "You see, there's no use trying to get the Commissioner. He's just a dummy."

"Whom would you suggest?"

"Mayor William T. Harding."

"Why?"

"Because he'll mean more, and because he's the figure-head, even if he does take orders like everybody else."

Again nobody said anything, until Portis startled them again by sitting up straight suddenly, and banging on his desk.

"Then, I say to you, Mr. Fitzhugh, go get the Mayor!"

Soon after, Dan and Grody left the big office.

Grody remarked: "You'll have to watch your step."

"It's kind of a lousy thing to do, Mike. Billy isn't such a bad guy."

"He's a rat," said Grody venomously.

"Yeah, but—anyway, I'll have a lot of fun. Those guys have walked all over me."

"Get the Mayor," Grody grinned.

CHAPTER II

Martinis, Bullets and Love

THAT night about nine, Dan left his room in the Berlin Hotel in Forty-ninth Street between Broadway and Eighth Avenue, and walked directly east to Park Avenue, where he entered a four-story brownstone front house. He rang the bell. The door opened a crack.

"Ah, good evening, Meester Feetzhugh!" The sleek-haired man behind the door opened it wider. Dan went in, shed his hat and coat into the hands of the check girl, whom he patted on the shoulder, and strolled into the front room where the window shades were down. Easy leather chairs and little wicker tables stood in groups around the walls. Behind that room, where Dan now went, was a tiny room with a ten-foot bar. Opposite the bar was a bench. Still beyond that room was another, like the front one. On the bench sat a girl, or woman, Dan never did make up his mind which.

She smiled when she saw him, and extended a beautifully-molded white arm. He took her hand, squeezed it momentarily, then dropped it.

"A scotch and soda," he said over his shoulder to the

bartender. Then he sat down beside Lila Bennett. "How's baby?"

She allowed her bare shoulder to touch his. He felt the soft flesh and liked her perfume. "I'm a little tired, Danny-boy."

"Cut the Danny-boy," he grinned. "I don't like it. Give me some dirt."

"Oh, I don't know!" Her white, smooth face grimaced, parting her redly moist lips, to allow Dan a glimpse of two rows of tiny white teeth, each looking as if it were pointed. He wanted to kiss her. "A lot of the bunch will be in tonight."

"I thought so. Billy? Helen?"

She nodded. "God, I'm exhausted. Last night a crowd of debs and college boys. Honest, they raise more hell than anybody. First families! First in the gutter."

"Don't tell about it. Why'n hell don't you close this joint and go away."

"With you, honey boy?"

"That's an idea."

"On your money, I suppose! I think you're one grand guy but—"

"You're liable to get in a stink here some time. It's messy."

"Don't make me laugh. With Mayor William T. Harding getting carried out of here cock-eyed at least once a week?"

"He's a God-damn' fool," said Dan off-handedly. "Last night, again? With Helen?"

"Two nights ago. I don't know how he can look at City Hall in the morning."

"He ought to have more sense than to walk all over with that Helen. She's—"

The front door opened and closed. A man's voice was heard kidding the hat girl.

"Firenze." Dan's face tightened.

He felt Lila's warm breath in his ear. "I like you to-night, Danny-boy. Stick around after the brawl."

"If I'm still on my feet."

Firenze came in—a short, stocky, swarthy man with a smooth, bland expression on his face. He wore dress clothes invariably after six o'clock, and that made his dark skin look darker. Confidential Secretary to the Mayor he was. His composure ruffled when he saw Dan and Lila together.

"Hello, Dan," he said easily. "And the beautiful lady."

"Little Albert." Lila smiled. "Is your boss coming, Albert?"

"Little while," the Italian growled, standing at the bar. "He has had a hard day."

"Of course," said Dan. "You too, I guess."

Firenze smiled. "I do not sit at a desk all day and look at papers. I have more important matters to attend to."

Dan smiled. "Why not attend to them?"

Lila laughed and put a hand on each one's arm. "You two little boys mustn't fight. I don't like my two best boy friends to fight. Because you *are* my two best boy friends."

Dan finished his drink, thinking that it was smart of her, if he only knew why, to feed the hate that existed between him and the Mayor's secretary.

Firenze's feelings got the better of him. "One of us must be the better."

"Hooey!" said Dan and walked into the back room.

As he walked there was sudden talking at the front door. A loud, jovial voice cried: "Hello, Lila, how's New York's darling? And Benny! Me old pal Benny. Warm, isn't it?" A female voice, not Lila's, giggled.

Dan turned and walked back into the bar room. The same voice cried: "Old Dan! Come on, sourface, how about Martinis all around?"

"Hello, Billy!" Dan greeted the Mayor. "How's things?"

"Great, wonderful, marvelous! Couldn't be better, could they, sweet?" He turned to the blonde girl hanging on his arm, smiling up at him steadily without special expression. Her evening dress was cut very low in the back, and loose, falling away now and then to reveal white flanks. In front, a tight bodice clung strategically to show the rising curve of breasts. Helen

Faire. Dan grinned at her, and wondered how Harding could stand her.

Martinis were ordered up all around, and Harding, his smart evening clothes accentuating the lines of his slim figure, became the center of a laughing, joking group. Dan looked with new eyes at the man he had been told to get. Brown hair went back from a rounded forehead, and thin eyebrows made almost straight lines above twinkling, genial hazel eyes. Narrow shoulders, a slim, well-kept figure for a man of forty-five, were all part of the man: impressive until the mouth became noticeable. Lips almost always parted in a sophisticated secret smile, but they were loose, and always gave Dan the impression of amiability verging on soft-headedness. An ingratiating personality that endeared itself to the public by taking nothing seriously, and that lent itself to the maneuvers of the master minds by taking orders with docility. Mayor William T. Harding of New York.

Helen screamed: "Come on, Billy, do that imitation of Al Jolson! Say, kids, wait'll you see this, it's a panic!"

Harding grinned. "Aw, not now, baby! Wait'll I get a few more in me. Then I'll do Al Jolson and Eddie Cantor combined. That's fair, isn't it, Dan?"

"Let's see what you can do." Dan had been looking at Lila, cooing in a corner with Firenze, who now and again looked sideways at Harding and then at Dan.

Helen said: "Aw, whadda ya wanna wait for?" Dan saw she had been having a few before they arrived there. She flung her bare arms around the Mayor's neck, and planted a noisy kiss on his cheek, leaving a blotch of rouge. Everybody laughed, and dove into the third round of Martinis. Harding paid every time.

Harding attacked Dan again: "Come on, cheer up, Danny. Your boss won't care. And if he does—poof!" He smiled, one hand stroking Helen's arm. His tongue wet his lips.

"Is he coming here?" Dan asked, taking another drink.

"He said he might stop in. But who wants his scowls now? God, I get 'em all day long over the phone. You don't blame me for this, do you?" He nodded toward Helen, who responded eagerly:

"Who's gonna blame my baby boy? Here, your glass's empty!" It seemed she couldn't talk without screaming. Dan knew how Harding had got her: by taking her away, an easy enough stunt, from a theatrical producer who had been building her up into a star. She had come along in musical shows a little faster with the Mayor behind her. She was suitable relaxation for the executive in his off hours, if he didn't go deaf in the meantime.

Dan took advantage of a little whispering between them to stroll over to Lila. Firenze had gone upstairs, where there were other rooms, with divans, pillows on the floor, a small piano, and other trappings of a secluded night life, including girls who came alone. Dan sat down:

"That dame gets on my nerves."

"Forget her. You're still sore about the wop."

"Why wouldn't I be? He's a worm. I don't like to be shoved around with him. Cut it out."

She smiled mysteriously. "Ooh—he's getting hard-boiled."

"What's your angle—mixing us two up together?"

"Can't you figure it?"

"If I could I wouldn't ask you. I won't tell you when I do."

"Woof!"

"I'll stick around tonight. But don't get the idea I'm excited about that bum. I don't have to stay here."

"No, you don't."

"So, that's it. See you anon." He got up and wandered back to the bar for another scotch. The Martinis were rotten and were giving him a headache. Harding, with about five cocktails under his ribs, slapped him on the back. His loose lips were glistening wet, and the blotch of rouge was still on his cheek. Helen had gone to the ladies' room.

"Dan, for Chris' sake, snap out of it! Y'd think ya lost y'r best pal." The hazel eyes were glassy and getting vague. The narrow shoulders drooped a little.

"I didn't lose any pal. I'm just tired, Billy. Tough day."

"Well, me too. Honest to God, I get so damn' sick of committees—I wish I didn't have the job o' being Mayor of this burg."

Dan said nothing.

The drink-loosened tongue went on: "Ya know, I guess you don't like Helen, but I'm tellin' ya that if I didn' have her to turn to, I'd damn well go nuts. Jesus, Bella drives me outa my mind! I don't know why the hell I married her. But at that she was a hot little baby before she got fat. Hell!" He pushed forward his glass for the bartender to fill. They were joined suddenly, quietly, by a little man, sleek, cat-footed, with shrewd blue eyes behind pince nez.

"Hello, chief!" Dan said. Harding pivoted slowly.

"Hello, Chollie! God, we got enough sourfaces here tanight. What the hell's wrong? Baby—" Helen walked back in, and ran to him as he called— "cheer these guys up."

She screwed her face up into a cute grimace, and stamped a foot. "Nassy ole men!" she pouted, and the Mayor roared.

Jessup smiled with tight lips. "Feeling pretty good, eh, Billy?" Texas born, he talked with a Southwestern accent.

"Have a drink. Benny, a Martini for Mr. Jessup!"

"No, Benny. Give me a straight scotch. I just came

from the office, and I've got a little headache. One of these and so to bed." The little, neat man downed his drink at a gulp. Then he turned to Dan: "Finish the Spiranzelli brief?"

Dan nodded. "This afternoon. It's tough, because the guy was guilty as hell."

"Yes, I know, but if we put up too good a case, the jury'll have to convict, and if that happens, we get that whole mob sore. Do what you can. Want to try it yourself in court?"

"Why not?"

They found one of Helen's arms about each of their necks. "Come on, you fussbudgets, drink up and let's have a real party! Helen wants ta get hot!"

Harding: "Come on, me lads! How about a real one? Lila, get some of the girls down!"

Lila joined them, smiling confidently at Dan, who shook his head just slightly. She said: "Billy, do me a favor and don't have a party here tonight. Besides, there isn't anybody here tonight you'd want on a party. Please, Billy!"

"I wanta party, I wanta party." Helen was getting cute. Dan and Jessup looked at each other. Dan looked past Lila and saw a new arrival in the doorway. "Billy, here's the Commissioner."

Harding again pivoted slowly to face the doorway. Commissioner of Police Francis Ollendorff towered in the opening. His hair stood up on his head like a military brush. His shoulders were stiffly back, and Dan pictured him suddenly in a Prussian Guards' officer's uniform. A black mustache hid Commissioner Ollendorff's upper lip, but left the lower, very thick one, visible. He stared haughtily around, picked out the Mayor, nodded quickly, and joined them. An unaccountable, dampening silence fell.

"Evening, Frank," somebody said. But the Commissioner didn't reply. He stared at Harding for a long time, until the smiling face became expressionless and wondering.

"Whassa matter, Frank?" asked Harding.

Ollendorff's startlingly high-pitched voice emerged from his spectacular bulk: "Can I talk to you gentlemen for a few minutes, privately?"

Dan caught Lila's eyes, raised his eyebrows, jerked his head to indicate an upstairs room. She broke in: "Frank, go upstairs to the front room. Albert is up there. Tell him to throw whoever's in there out."

The Commissioner of Police considered her briefly, then, without a further word, goose-stepped out of the bar and upstairs. In a minute, Dan followed, then Jessup, then Harding last. All unobtrusively, quietly, until the five of them sat on divans and pillows in a black and silver room.

Ollendorff spoke: "This matter is important. I didn't want to phone and I thought you fellows ought to know what has happened before we tell Walters."

Harding's facial expressions informed Dan how hard the Mayor was trying to get Martinis out of his head. Jessup said briskly:

"This is the devil of a way to give out news, Frank. In a speakeasy."

"Well, what do you expect? I didn't want to telephone." Ollendorff grew petulant. Jessup shrugged. Firenze smoked in a corner and listened.

The big man went on in a lower voice: "This is what happened. I just had a call from Miami. Fatty Stein was shot and killed there tonight."

Everybody waited in sudden tenseness. "Who by?" asked Dan.

The hulk frowned. "What's the difference? But this makes a different picture. What'll we do now about Carmody?"

Dan realized, or felt instinctively, that the Commissioner was rattled. Somebody had taken it upon himself to avenge Rosenberg's murder—without orders from the inside. The Commissioner, who had obtained his training as head of a huge interstate bus line, was scared.

Jessup cut in briskly: "No use our talking about it. Have we got all the facts?"

"There was a banquet or dinner going on in a roadhouse. Stein was there. Three men, masked, walked in and filled him with bullets. Simple, wasn't it? And damned annoying."

"This is no time to get annoyed," Jessup snapped. "What do you think we had better do, Billy?"

Harding slowly brought his gaze to bear on the District Attorney. Then he looked away. He was trying to get his thoughts together. Finally he chuckled. "I don't see why you guys think this is serious. Forget it. Fatty's dead, Rosenberg's dead. We're in the bag."

Firenze was watching Harding. Ollendorff scowled. Jessup took it up again: "Billy, have some sense. We don't know yet if it's serious. We've got to say something in the morning, though. We'd all better get together on this."

Dan put in: "I'll call Walters." He went out of the room and downstairs to a soundproof booth. He got Judge Walters's lugubrious tones over the wire: "What's that? You want to see me tonight? I'm just going to bed."

Dan explained: "It might be important. I'll call the others, and we'll be there in half an hour."

Then, in order, he called Tom Tully, district leader, and Max Dietrich and Henry Calloway, Hall sachems and district leaders. This was going to be a master mind session for fair. Then he went back upstairs. There Harding was arguing with Ollendorff, who said as Dan reëntered:

"I talked with the Chief of Police in Havana the other day and told him to drive Fatty over to Miami.

We didn't want him in Cuba, but I had no idea he would be killed."

"Maybe you will have to let Carmody go," said Firenze gently.

Jessup looked at him, startled: "What?"

Dan remarked easily: "Let the big guys figure it out, Wop."

The Italian's eyes flamed.

Dan went on: "You gotta try Carmody now, because you can't admit you knew all along that Fatty did for Rosenberg."

"There are other ways," said Jessup. "We can postpone the trial." But Dan knew he was thinking that if it could be stalled long enough, there would be a new District Attorney the first of the year to handle the messy business.

"Let's go," suggested Ollendorff.

Harding passed his hand over his forehead. "That shoots my party to hell."

Downstairs Helen seized him by the arm. "Come on, Billy!"

He patted her hand. "Party's off, kid. Phone you tomorrow. You go home now and sleep alone." Somebody laughed.

She flung off into the bar. Harding sighed, put on his coat and rakish felt hat, and went out into the street. Dan was the last to leave, when Jessup said: "I guess it's okay for you to come, Dan. I want one of my boys there." They stared at each other and Dan nodded. Jessup preceded him, when he found Lila close beside him.

"Coming back, Dan?"

"We might be all night." He glanced at her. She looked very desirable. He thought of Firenze, shrugged, and said: "If it's not too late I'll be back in a few hours. Or I'll phone."

She kissed him quickly, with open mouth. He went out.

CHAPTER III

His Master's Voice

THE Mayor's car and a taxicab brought them all to
Judge Andrew Jackson Walters's home in Abingdon
Square. A man-servant led them to the library, and
Walters came in after a moment. His gigantic, well-
proportioned body sank easily into an armchair and the
swarthy face, with its features seemingly hacked out of
wood, turned an imposing mask toward the visitors.
Here, reflected Dan scornfully, was the great false-
front which had been set up after Boss Brophy's death
to sell the sentimental public the idea of a "better Hall".

Walters's brown eyes were fixed in a sullen stare.
His voice was low and monotonous, which was his idea
of being quietly masterful.

Ollendorff started to talk: "The point is, Andy,
Fatty Stein was bumped tonight in Miami."

The brown eyes lighted up in sudden excitement.
"Ha!"

Harding sat tranquilly by, Firenze beside him, smoking. Before they got any further Tully came in. Dan
figured him as the coming strong man, and he looked
it. Honest Tom was his nickname, and it was well de-

served. While most of the boys dipped their fingers in sideline profits, Tully never touched any of that because he was too smart—and independently wealthy. He had the will to power, had a brain better than anybody else's when it came to district and city politics, and was a clever manipulator of men. Dan admired him as he would admire a remarkable machine. He liked the benevolent look that Tully's fifty-year-old face wore. He liked the subdued clothes, the low, powerful voice and expressionless mouth.

Honest Tom Tully greeted Judge Walters casually and sat down to light a cigar. He sat quietly until Calloway and Dietrich arrived: both men of distinguished bearing, bank directors and realtors on the side, their real business being the administration of the Hall. They played together and were reasonable allies for any move that looked like the advancement of the organization. They were smarter than Walters, but not strong. Their names reached the public only on such occasions as the Hall held an election within itself, or in their business capacities. Dan had expected Lewis Duffy, secretary to the Hall, to be here with Calloway, but obviously he didn't figure in this session.

When everybody had arrived who was going to arrive, Tully—not Walters—said:

"What's this all about?"

They left it to Ollendorff: "Stein was bumped in Miami tonight."

"You told us that already," said Walters.

"I'll give you the facts of it," the Commissioner began, but Honest Tom cut in:

"Do you, or anybody else, know who did it?"

Ollendorff said: "We can guess. I will put a special squad of men on the job, and—"

Walters's rumbling voice threw in hastily: "That's a lot of nonsense, Ollendorff. Either we know or we don't. Your dumb detectives won't find out anything we don't know already."

The Big Noise exploded in words: "I don't see how you can say that! I've built up the Department along very efficient lines and—"

"If we know who did it, we'll keep on knowing. If we don't, it doesn't make much difference. We can make guesses, anyway, pretty accurately," Tully explained patiently. "What's your slant, Charlie?"

"I don't know anything about it, but it sounds to me like a job by some of Rosenberg's enemies. I doubt if the killing has any more significance than that some of the people on that damned list got rattled. They concluded Stein had the list, and decided to take no chances," Jessup replied.

"Maybe," said Tully. "What's yours, Billy?"

"Huh?" queried Harding, frowning. Then he brightened: "I think we ought to be glad he's dead, just on general principles. Let's forget the whole damn thing."

He sneaked a look at his wrist watch. Tully made no reply, but turned hopefully to Calloway:

"Henry, *you* talk sense."

The lean, black-haired man—over sixty, Dan knew—considered. Then he spoke slowly and carefully:

"I think it doesn't much matter who killed Stein. We know he didn't have that list, whoever else may have it. Besides, we aren't the only ones who know that Stein killed Rosenberg, nor the only ones who know he didn't have the list. What we have to decide, very definitely now, is what to do about Carmody."

Jessup chirped: "My idea exactly."

Dan allowed himself a mental grin. Carmody was getting to be a white elephant on everybody's hands, even though Jessup didn't know how big a one on his own.

Dietrich, with efficient Prussian blood in his veins, contributed: "I agree with Henry, Tom. We were every one of us of a mind that Rosenberg's dying so opportunely was a matter of congratulation all around. In view of the circumstances, it struck me as a much more difficult matter not to catch the murderer than to catch him."

"Crandall thought so, too," Tully commented.

Dan knew what he meant, because the former Police Commissioner Crandall, in his eagerness to please the master minds, had done a poor job of failing to solve the murder. Which was why Walters, heavily influ-

enced by Tully, had forced Harding to dismiss the
wizened ex-lawyer and put in the ex-bus executive.

Silence fell on them all. Harding sat quiet, obviously
waiting to be told what to do. Dan felt surge up in him
a sudden contemptuous loathing for this man who had
so little intelligence to apply to his job. They had
picked a mere figure-head, all right! Dan looked at his
own superior, who had Carmody on his hands without
knowing what to do with him. In Charles Jessup they
had a smart man, but at times difficult to handle. Which
was why they had unloaded Carmody on him—to kill
him off politically unless he turned up some whiz of an
idea.

Ollendorff sat sullenly after having been squelched
by Tully. Walters broke the thinking spell:

"My idea is that Carmody ought to be tried either
now, or after this year's mayoralty election."

This was so obvious, nobody said anything. Dan wondered that Tully was at so little pains to conciliate
Walters, who until recently had had powerful backing
in the organization. Clearly Tully himself saw that
Walters was rattled by the way things were going—
painless though it was—and knew also that when that
became a little more generally known, Walters was
through.

The head of the Hall went on: "There's altogether
too much fuss being made about not finding who killed
Rosenberg, and we've got to do something. The Big

Fellow was saying—" Then he stopped and darted a worried sidelong look at Tully, who said very slowly:

"I don't think it's at all necessary to worry about what Jim White says. He doesn't carry much weight any more, as I have told him."

Dan believed that last, even though White, ex-Governor of the State and defeated candidate for President, was in every way the equal, and in many ways the superior, of Tully, particularly in political power in the city. Everybody figured that White was through, so much so that he never sat in on any of the lesser Hall conferences, participating only in the big ones that got into the papers.

Tully kept talking, and his tone made it clear that this was orders. Walters, his face resentful, listened like the rest.

"We'll put the Carmody trial off till the Fall. That's easy, because the court calendars are known to be crowded, and Frank Ollendorff needs more time to collect evidence."

"If that's the case," Walters put in, "I think it would be better to keep Carmody in jail for at least three months more."

"I object to that," Jessup said. "We've got to make a pretense at fairness here, and sooner or later somebody, knowing Carmody never did it, will complain at his being shut up."

"I insist he remain in jail!" Walters protested. "Suppose he should run away?"

Harding suddenly said, anxious to remain in things: "I don't think he'd do that."

Ollendorff reinforced him: "We'll see that he doesn't!"

Tully said: "I think he should be released on bail." "I won't have it!"

Calloway and Dietrich, smart enough to know Walters's power, but perhaps not cagey enough to play with Tully, agreed verbally, though not very emphatically, with the Judge.

Tully's eyes gleamed, but he gave in: "All right. Then it's this way: Charlie, you find when Carmody can be tried, in the Fall, but don't announce it yet. Keep a tentative date in mind. Frank, you see if you can find out who did in Stein, just for the sake of curiosity."

"We'll know within two weeks!"

"I hope so," said Jessup and Ollendorff glared. Dan caught Tully looking appraisingly at Ollendorff.

Dietrich's cold voice was heard again: "We were all glad to see Rosenberg go. None of us regrets Stein's passing. But I do think we ought to learn what happened to that list."

Tully got worried now. "I've said this before, and I say it again, that some of you—" Dan knew he meant Harding, but Honest Tom didn't specify—"ought to be a bit more discreet. If that list ever gets out, it will be very unpleasant. Mind you, no one, Judge Walters, myself, or anyone else, is at all concerned with the thing in a personal way. We are interested in the political implications. Remember, gentlemen, we are in many ways a political organization. Personal scandal, however, is very harmful politically. There are people who believe that scandal has no place in political campaigns, but we know that it has. I don't blame anyone for doing away with political reputations as best they can. If people think you are a bad family man, they will not think the better of you as a Commissioner of Accounts, or any other job. This is a point to remember. Also, that is why the Rosenberg list is important."

Everybody listened carefully, but said nothing when he finished. Firenze looked at his own employer, who looked at the floor. Everybody else was expressionless, because they all suspected, even if nobody was sure, that Harding, among others, was on the Rosenberg list as a borrower of money. Tully flicked his cigar, and cleared his throat to indicate that he was finished. Harding leaned back in his chair and inspected the ceiling. He cleared his throat and said:

"All right, but we don't know where the list is. But we do know we've got Carmody, and now we've settled he's to be tried right after the elections."

Jessup broke in: "You know, I wouldn't mind his coming up sooner."

Tully made an impatient face. "No, Charlie. I know you've got the unpleasant job of making this look like a real trial. But we must not have Carmody getting off scot free at a time when his release can be used against us. That's clear, isn't it?" Jessup said no more the rest of the session.

Walters's heavy voice boomed on: "Now we've got to make sure what Billy's to say from now on if the complaints get any stronger. Nobody else will let it out that Stein was the one who—"

Dietrich stood up and crossed the room to flick his cigar ash in the fireplace. There he turned and looked around. "It strikes me that it won't be necessary for Billy to say anything about this. All we want to do is make up our own minds."

Calloway nodded, Tully listened approvingly. The German continued with thoroughness: "We are glad that Rosenberg went, because he was a most unpleasant person, neither completely identified with any of the gangs, nor with anyone else. Stein was of no special importance, except as the real culprit in case of need. But in general, Rosenberg's death was convenient and harmed no one. Therefore Stein was not taken in. We would not have the present—ah—awkward situation but for two little items: the missing list and Crandall's lamentable mishandling of the pursuit of Carmody. So lamentable that Carmody thought best to give himself up. With that we are all familiar."

Harding's voice, showing the huskiness of the Martinis worn off, cut in: "We talked this all over a hundred times."

But Dietrich went on smoothly: "I am merely running over the salient points of our attitude so that all of us are agreed and in harmony. Now—we have left only two things: to make the Carmody trial seem vigorous, but fruitless because the murder was not solvable, and second, to keep its result from interfering with the elections next Fall. That is your job, Jessup."

The D.A. nodded.

Dietrich started to go on, but Tully took it up: "Now that brings us to something that's been on my mind for some time. Andy, you remember we talked about this several weeks ago. It's this, gentlemen: we want a new figure at our head—" Walters's eyes jumped—"in place of Jim White."

Dan admired Tully more. He was smooth, but direct, or seemed to be, which came to the same thing.

"Why?" asked Calloway.

Honest Tom shrugged. "Jim and I have talked about this, and I can tell you it was very unpleasant for both of us. But the fact remains that he is no longer, politically speaking, the man he was. I feel that as a State leader he is no longer valuable to us. In a matter of this sort, gentlemen, we can't afford to be sentimental."

Everybody thought fast. This was daring, but necessary. Dan doubted whether Tully had really put it up to the Big Fellow that he was through; but anyway, Tully believed himself strong enough to raise the question. It took courage, even at an informal meeting like this one, and Dan respected him for it. Tully went on:

"As I see it, Judge Walters is not the man, for the simple reason that the leader of the Hall, without public following, wouldn't be well received by the papers. The rest of us are out for various reasons. My idea is Billy."

Nobody commented on that. It took their breaths away. Harding, it was well-known, largely owed the mayoralty to Jim White's influence, but had lost the Big Fellow's confidence by his frivolous public behavior in office. It would be a terrible slap at White to try to set up Billy Harding in his place as State leader. Tully felt their thoughts, because he picked up again explanatorily:

"Now, stop a minute and think this over. In Billy we've got a man with marvelous personality, and enormous popularity in the city. It only remains for us to build him in the State. Why not?"

Harding protested: "I think you're going too fast, even if White is through."

Calloway rapped: "We need somebody with your slant. Besides, Jim was difficult sometimes. Washington caught his eye."

"Nothing like that for Billy Harding," Ollendorff laughed, trying to be jovial. Firenze did the Mayor's glaring for him. Dan grinned openly at Tully.

Dietrich spoke: "I have suspected something of the sort was in your mind, Tom. That is why I spoke as I did before. Billy will do, but he's got to know how to behave."

"Hell—" said Harding. He stood up and walked into

the middle of the room. "Listen to me a minute. You fellows sit around and decide what's going to happen. Maybe I can give you a little different picture."

"Go on," Calloway urged.

"I think you take this Carmody business too seriously. This won't be the first murder that wasn't solved, even if it did cause a row. Why make such a fuss about it? Suppose Carmody is acquitted, as he will be, and a lot of people think we ought to have sent him up despite his innocence, haven't we still got the organization?" He felt better now; he had the center of the room, and though he wasn't talking sense, he thought he was.

Dan got up courage to talk. "Pardon me if I butt in, but it seems to me that the Carmody business is a whole lot *more* important than any of you think."

Walters growled: "So? Show me."

Dan went on, shooting a side glance at Jessup, who watched with what Dan thought was approval: "I happen to know that a whole lot of people are sore about the Carmody trial postponement. We want to put up a big fight on it, and then we'll still have the organization to fall back on."

"He talks sense," somebody said, Dan didn't know who. He leaned back and shut up, satisfied. Harding looked at him uncertainly, then smiled and nodded.

Tully again summed up: "Billy, take it from us, this is serious if only because it's not a one-man job.

We're all in it. In the campaign, the mess can be blamed on us, unofficially, on you as Mayor, on the District Attorney's office, on the courts, on everybody. Then there's the list—"

Harding lost his patience: "Stop squawking about that list! Whoever's got it would have done something with it before this if they wanted to, wouldn't they?"

Walters remarked: "Maybe. But listen, Billy, forget all that now. We're decided on all those angles. The main point is that you're the mouthpiece now. You do the talking for all of us."

"Let's not get excited," suggested the Police Commissioner, looking bewildered. Firenze watched Dan quietly, because it was clear the conference was nearing its end.

Tully got up and stretched. "So don't say anything about anything yet. There's plenty of politics to be played this summer and fall." And he let his cold mouth split in a smile. Somebody coughed, and everybody knew Tully came off number one, Walters number two, and that Harding would listen to Tully.

The conversation spread to personalities and generalities. Jessup and Dan slipped out, Harding and Firenze behind them.

Dan heard the Mayor complain: "I'll be a little late in the morning."

Dan hailed a cab, bade his chief good-by, and drove off down the street. Then he gave the driver Lila's address. His watch said two-thirty. He yawned and lit a cigarette.

CHAPTER IV

Lila's Bedtime Story

THERE were still customers in the bar when Dan got back there. Lila wasn't visible, so he questioned Benny.

"She's upstairs with a headache," the man told him. "Said for you to come up if you got here by now."

Dan nodded, had a whisky and soda to clear his own head, and then strolled out when nobody was looking. He ascended two flights of steps, and stopped before a heavy, silver-painted door on the third floor. He pushed a buzzer and waited. In ten seconds Lila opened to him, and let him in with a smile. He skimmed his hat across the room and dropped his coat on a footstool.

"Well?" she asked.

"Nothing except what you'd expect. Let's talk about something else."

She sank on a chaise longue, smoking a cigarette. "You're in a filthy mood."

He stared at her, the light from the standing lamp behind her throwing a soft golden radiance over her negligeed figure. He liked Lila, and smiled. "No, I'm not, kiddo. But a lot of words get tiresome. What's new?"

"Nothing. Sit down. There's whisky on the table, and ice and soda. I'm tired." She extinguished her cigarette, got up and crossed the room slowly, passing a hand over her forehead. The sleeve of her negligee fell back to her shoulder. Dan caught her in his arms as she passed and found her mouth under his. She looked up at him lazily between narrowed lids. "You're rough."

"Don't ritz me." Her body was soft and yielding in his arms. He released her, and went over to have a drink. She turned, slipped off her negligee and climbed into the wide, silken-coverleted bed on the other side of the dim room. Dan swallowed some of his drink and looked at her.

"Firenze just phoned," she said.

He crossed to beside the bed and looked down at her. "What did he want?"

She smiled maliciously. "Still burning up? He wanted to drop in for a chat."

He drank some more. "No, I'm not burning up. I don't have to, even if I do like you."

"You're stuck on yourself."

His hand strayed over her shoulder. "No, I'm not. But I don't like competition from that dog-robber."

She turned her head away. "My head aches."

He finished his drink, got into pajamas and lit another cigarette as he squatted on the side of the bed. "I have to get up early."

"Well, go to bed."

"I'm wide awake. Got plenty thinking to do this summer."

She sat up suddenly, animatedly: "You know, I've been thinking all evening—that Helen."

He smoked steadily. "What about her?"

"You're real pally with Billy, aren't you?" Lila was intent.

"So-so."

"Anyway, tell him to get rid of her. There'll be trouble with her yet. He should have held on to Madeleine."

Dan said nothing. She went on: "She'll get him in trouble, you mark my words."

He waved a hand. "She doesn't know anything that would really hurt him if it got out. Besides, what she means is personal dirt, and you know the Christers are too righteous to let stuff like that have any importance."

"Personal dirt, is it?" Lila lay back and tousled her hair. "You think it's only that?"

"Isn't it? What do you know?"

"Oh, I guess maybe you're right. She just talks too much about him."

Dan made up his mind she did know something, and he had inadvertently scared her off. He changed his methods. Before saying anything, he lay back beside her and stared up at the ceiling. "She boozes an awful lot."

Lila was silent, then burst out: "Honest, it gets me

sometimes! You know me—I know a few of the facts of life, and I served my time in dressing rooms that make Eugene O'Neill sound like a prayer book." Dan smoked on. "But that girl raises the hair on my head. The stories she tells about 'me and Billy', you wouldn't believe 'em!"

"Certainly I would," he grinned.

"Hm. I guess *you* would! I'm hard-boiled, but she makes their love scenes sound like—like— He ought to put a muffler on her! Where she learned her language God only knows. The Mayor should have a better girl than that cluck."

"You, maybe," he suggested tonelessly.

"That's what you think! But I'd be ashamed to tell such stories about any man I was with. Oh, well, I'll spare you the sordid details. But if it ever gets to the papers—"

"They don't print stuff like that. Besides, you can't prove it. It sounds too much like lies, even if it is true."

"Maybe they can't prove that. But she knows, and talks about plenty that can be proved."

"I think he's too smart to gab, even in his frequent cups." He modulated his tone very carefully.

She bit. "You wise lawyers!" She was even contemptuous. "Because you tell me things, you think nobody else does!"

"I tell you lots of things," he conciliated.

She leaned up on one elbow and stared belligerently

down at him: "Then match this: he told who was on the Rosenberg list."

He didn't hide his surprise. "Hell 'n' Mary!"

"I tell you they're both clowns and it's up to you to put him wise. He's on the list for a big sock of money. Some magistrates are on it—I don't remember the names."

"I wish you did." Dan's heart pumped. This was hot.

Lila's white forehead wrinkled. He took her hand and kissed it in the palm. She said slowly: "One of the names was Belgar, Helgar—something like that."

"Belgar, it is," he corrected her. "That's interesting. Think of some more." He wanted to keep her from stopping to consider. She went on: "Then an Italian name this goof remembered. Name some wop magistrates."

"There's only a few," he told her, thinking fast. "Balbaterri in Brooklyn some place; Pasquale, and—"

Her hand dropped on his chest. "That's the one! Pasquale."

"Any more?"

Lila sighed. "I can't remember. She was drunk the other night and spilled all this."

"Why? You her special pal, or something? Be hell if she got wise you were after li'l Billy."

"I'm not, you damned fool, but I don't want the wretch sore at me. That's easy."

"She's silly, I guess," and he yawned, more from excitement than weariness.

"God, is she! You know what else she told me?" Lila was forgetting her headache. "She told me how when he was supposed to be on vacation some quiet place, he was really in Montreal with her. 'We were cock-eyed', she screams. What if that sort of thing gets out?"

"Yeah. What else?"

Lila fell back on her pillow. "Oh, a lot more talk. Told me how she sneaked Billy away from Madeleine."

"That so?"

"Well, you know all that."

They both fell silent. Her hand sought his and she sighed in sudden sleepiness. He asked: "Why pick on me to spill this to? What about the wop secretary?"

"He's too stupid."

"I don't know about that. Billy thinks more of him than he does of me."

"Wrong again, big boy. Billy really likes you a lot. Helen told me that, too. God, I wish she didn't get so chatty."

"What did she do, get this way all of a sudden?"

"No. It's been this way for weeks, maybe months."

"Well, why in hell did you——"

"I know. Why didn't I tell you before? Because she only let that about the names out the other night. I haven't seen you—up here—since."

"That's right. But you could have told the wop."

Her hand detached itself from his and slapped him. He laughed. She went on, her voice getting drowsy:

"I can't tell him stuff like that. He gets excited, and he's dangerous."

"Why to you?"

He felt her bare shoulders move in a shrug. "But that's on the level about Billy liking you. He thinks well of you, the dope told me. Your father was his wet nurse, or something."

"I'd never know he felt that way."

"Well, he does. Now forget it and go to sleep." She fell silent, and he stared thoughtfully up over his head. This was a big evening. The personal scandal that might have spread through Helen's careless conversation didn't worry him, and wouldn't worry anybody else, but the list tidbit was a bull's-eye.

He wondered what Harding could be thinking of, not to be scared at that list floating around New York. Suppose a newspaper got hold of it before anybody knew of it? Dan breathed deep. He thought back earlier in the evening, when Tully had broadcast his general warning, and Harding had told them to stop worrying over the list. Dan felt a renewal of his contempt at the man's utter self-confidence. Or was it that? Well, they were all confident nothing could seriously harm them.

But Harding must have some idea of where the list had gone. There weren't many people who would be apt to know it existed, before Rosenberg's safe had been examined by Brand and his men. Dan figured it over carefully, and forgot all about Lila lying next to him, her breath coming softly and slowly.

The list was only good for two things: for publication by a newspaper, or for use in the next campaign by some opposition candidate. Or else Stein had had it, but Dan doubted that very much. Stein was small fry, and the list was too much dynamite for a gun to work to advantage. Dynamite was the word. It might blow them all to Kingdom Come.

The odds were against a paper having it, just on the face of probability. The odds were for the opposition having got hold of it by rifling the safe. Maybe Harding was doing some undercover sleuthing on his own hook, and that was why he wasn't worried. Maybe— maybe—maybe—if—if—if! Dan pursed his lips in annoyance. It struck him, also, that even if a newspaper did have the thing, they wouldn't use it because of the big society names on it. Maybe, maybe not. There might be an angle there, but it all depended on exactly who was on the roster. Dan couldn't see any immediate use for his knowledge. He couldn't give it to Portis, because the old boy would blow up with excitement and spring the works too soon. Somebody else had to do it. And then—maybe—these two girls had the thing mixed up. But on last thought, that wasn't likely.

Anyway, Dan began to feel as if he had a touchy grenade up his sleeve. There was going to be plenty of fun, and it had already been a full day. A thought struck him, and he said suddenly:

"Baby!"

Lila made a faint groaning sound.

"Hey! Wake up!"

She turned over protestingly and faced him sleepily. He grinned indulgently and ran one hand over her hair. A waft of its odor came to him. "Listen, sweet, don't spill this to the wop."

"I told you I wouldn't," she grumbled.

"I know, I know, but this is hot enough stuff to put us all away."

"You can count on me, Dan."

"Like hell I will. Listen, sweetheart, if you drop a word of this to anybody—this is a friendly tip—I'll close this joint up and send you up."

"Oh, you're a lousy rat!" she flared, awake again, with anger.

He shook her by the shoulder. "Never mind that. I mean business. Just remember you told me, and nobody else. If the wop thought you knew this, he'd put you away with bullets."

"Oh, not that parlor gangster!"

"Think you can handle him, eh?"

She smiled secretly, seductively.

"All right. But just on general principles you better put a keep-out sign on the door for him."

"No. I like him."

"You heard what I said, baby. I mean it. One word, and Federal boys'll be up to take you over to the island."

Her white arms crept around his neck. "You wouldn't

do that, to me, Danny, would you?" He wasted no opportunities. He kissed her hard on the lips. She went on: "You wouldn't do it to me! I'm crazy about you, Danny!"

"That's got nothing to do with it."

She pulled his head over closer beside hers and pressed her warm lips against his ear. "Oh, yes, it has!"

He disengaged himself. "The hell I won't do it."

"Then I'll keep quiet," she submitted suddenly and dropped sullenly back on her pillow. He smiled. She was swell, but he didn't want to trust anybody. "You're a sweet," he said.

She pouted. "You're in a great mood tonight."

"I think I'm charming," he grinned, feeling very triumphant. "I just don't want you to talk."

"I won't! You ought to know me well enough."

"How do I know what you tell that garlic-grower?"

"You never heard of anything."

"No—o. Well, anyway, let's forget it. We've got dynamite under us. Just remember that."

"You don't seem very excited." Lila was again lazily seductive.

He subtly switched the topic. "I can be excited without looking it."

She made an inarticulate sound. Then she said as if to herself: "I wouldn't mind having a boy friend who wasn't mixed up with all this mob. I think they're dangerous."

Dan said nothing more. He felt he had learned all he was going to learn, and that was plenty for one day. He experienced a strange intoxication, the lift of triumph. In his mind there suddenly formed a desire to tell Lila that he was out to get the Mayor. He couldn't get out of himself—hadn't been able to all day—the furtive feeling that he was sticking a knife in somebody's back. Harding's, maybe, if he looked at it that way. Or maybe he was just removing a knife from between his own ribs. He decided to look at it that way and on top of that he conquered the almost insuperable desire to tell somebody—Lila. She moved softly against him, and he put the whole thing out of his brain, deliberately letting his mind revel in its feeling of triumph at the dope he had picked up. After all, no one but himself would ever understand why he wasn't a rat to turn in a rat. He stretched and sighed and lit a final cigarette.

"Aren't you ever going to stop smoking?" Lila's voice drooped off into drowsiness.

He smoked on till half the cigarette was gone, then he squashed it in an ash tray and pulled the little gold chain of the bedside lamp.

Lila murmured: "My Danny-boy."

"Yeah."

CHAPTER V

A Check for a Grand

COLONEL PORTIS' sexless secretary knew Dan for a repeated, if not frequent, caller after hours at the Wall
Street office. He couldn't elicit a smile from her, but
she showed him in, late one afternoon in June, without
announcing him over the interoffice phone. He walked
in quickly, wishing he didn't ever have to come here,
because it was dangerous. But something special was in
the wind. The moment he stepped on the thick carpet
beyond the doorway, he saw a man he recognized:
George De Angelis, member of the House of Representatives from a New York City district. A thick,
squat, belligerent-looking man with a shock of black
hair that seemed never to have been combed, he sat in
the chair on the opposite side of the desk from that on
which Dan usually sat.

Portis shook hands with Dan. "Good afternoon, my
boy. How are you?"

"I'm still alive, Colonel. Can't expect much more."

The old gentleman smiled. "No, I suppose not." But
he wasn't thinking what Dan was thinking. His res-

onant, authoritative voice rolled on: "Of course, you know Representative De Angelis. This is the Mr. Fitzhugh I told you about."

Dan thought harshly of the Colonel for doing so much talking. He said: "Never met before, I don't believe. How are you?"

The shock-headed man was standing up. He shook hands fiercely. Dan soon noticed that he did everything fiercely, and laid it to his Italian blood. Dan sat down, but De Angelis said to the Colonel:

"Is there a private office here I could use for a moment? There's a call I'd like to make, and—"

"Of course, of course!" The financier pushed a buzzer; the sexless secretary materialized in the doorway. "Miss Peabody, take Mr. De Angelis to one of the other offices—a telephone call—yes." The Congressman went out in the secretary's wake.

Dan looked at the Colonel, who began right away: "I am glad of this moment of privacy, although I did want you to meet and talk to him."

Dan waited.

"Before we go on to other matters, I want to express to you how gratified I am at your work. I feel—and other members of our organization feel also—that we are at length on the point of arriving somewhere. We are waging a long and thus far silent fight, but I view the future with considerable—"

Dan cut in: "I haven't done anything tangible yet."

"Ah, I know that, of course! But the moment is not far off?"

Dan shook his head. In some ways, the Colonel baffled him. The banker had periodically given him installments of the promised one hundred thousand dollars —bills in a long envelope, and no witnesses—in return for Dan's merely telling him things. Dan concluded he looked a great deal more honest than he thought he did. So far, he had given the Colonel no documentary evidence whatever, and he was rapidly forming the opinion that the Colonel could do just as well without that sort of dynamite. Papers got lost too easily, and were too traceable. He could tell enough things, if they happened, to satisfy Portis. Knowledge was more important than scraps of paper.

"I am glad you think that the time is approaching when we may strike the first blow. For I—we—have thought so, too. City-wide primaries are coming in September."

Dan lit a cigarette.

"I have wanted to ask you, but the last time I saw you there were so many other matters—precisely what significance does the change in the leadership of the Hall have?" The Colonel was at least less trusting than he had been months before, when he would have believed that a new leader of the Hall merely meant a new organizer of clambakes.

Dan explained quickly, wanting to get it over before

the impetuous Italian returned: "It's about a month now, and we're all getting used to Tully. I thought we talked about that. It means several things."

"Suppose you just give me a brief outline of how it happened." And the old gentleman who was going to purify New York City government leaned back in his chair.

Dan leaned forward and talked fast. "Here it is. Walters was through insofar as influence in the organization went. Dietrich and Calloway are smart enough to follow the real leader, particularly when he's good. Tully is smarter than all of them except Jim White, who lost his organization backing last Presidential elections. So they made it so tough for Walters, paid no attention to him, that he was forced out. They as much as told him to go. Somebody suggested White as next leader, but the insiders laughed that off. Plenty of them would like to stick knives into him anyway. Lots of others came into the picture, but in the end Honest Tom got it. Meantime Walters took himself a trip for his health. Said he had jaundice. Maybe he really did. What it means—" Dan wondered if the Colonel grasped all he was spouting so swiftly— "what it means is that Harding has a stronger boss now. He had him before, but not so directly. Tully has guts, is a much better politician, and carries more weight. That's all."

The Colonel nodded, digesting what he had heard. "So that we may expect exactly what—?"

"You can expect Harding to be renominated in the primaries. There'll be a new District Attorney and a new—"

The door behind Dan opened with a subdued click, and Dan went right on: "And I believe I'll take my vacation in about two months' time. Yes, I—" De Angelis was beside them again, sitting down. Portis stared at Dan, then a twinkle of amusement came in his blue eyes. The fiery Italian said:

"Thank you very much for the use of the phone."

The Colonel raised a courtly hand. "Now for the real business of the day, Mr. Fitzhugh."

Dan relaxed in his chair. De Angelis, he felt, was examining him carefully and furtively.

"I have told Mr. De Angelis that in your capacity of Assistant District Attorney you are in a position to understand many difficult things about city politics. Is that not so? Now, we—that is, the People's Franchise Union and many other prominent men—are thinking of inducing Mr. De Angelis to run for Mayor."

Dan kept his face expressionless. This was a new angle.

"So, the question is this, and I want your frank opinion: do you believe Mr. De Angelis can be nominated for Mayor on an independent ticket?"

"To run him as an independent, all you need to do is to get up a petition with so many thousand signatures of voters. That would be easy," replied Dan, as if he were teaching a class in political kindergarten. "But Mr. De Angelis is a Republican. To attract any attention, he would have to carry the Republican primaries. First and foremost, he must be the regular nominee of his own party. After that, the independent tag can be hung on him too."

Both men nodded: "Could he, then, if nominated in the Republican primaries, be elected to the Mayoralty?"

Dan did not feel it at all necessary to think twice. "Never!" he said.

They both looked a little startled at his directness. He was moved to dilate:

"I mean: it may be possible, by energetic campaigning—which costs a hell of a lot of money—and by having something very hot to campaign about—to get Mr. De Angelis nominated by the Republicans. I scarcely need to tell you that the G.O.P. conservatives regard him as little better than a Socialist. But if he does carry his party primaries, it'll take a lot more than that to lick the Democratic candidate and the Tammany vote. That's what I mean. But something else is possible. . . ."

The Colonel raised his eyebrows in query.

Dan dropped slowly: "It's possible for Mr. De Angelis to raise an unholy row. Raise it—at least start one."

"How?" injected De Angelis, leaning suddenly forward, and putting one clenched fist on the desk top. His small dark eyes bored at Dan.

"Just this way," said Dan. "Tell 'em that Magistrate Antonio Pasquale was one of those who borrowed money from Al Rosenberg, gambler, deceased."

The Colonel started talking at once: "Why, Mr. Fitzhugh, I fail to see how that unfortunate fact—disgraceful, I had better say, could be of any value—"

But De Angelis, after a moment's surprise, was on his feet. "Pasquale one of the— By God, that's tremendous!" But he didn't look glad.

Dan hadn't far to guess for that reason. He grinned and remarked: "Too bad one of the few Italian magistrates had to be it."

The little stocky man took a deep breath. His black eyes glittered. "This is infamous!"

Portis said in a tone of quiet horror: "The man is undoubtedly a crook!"

De Angelis: "Crook! That's just one part of it!" He turned on Dan. "Go ahead. Explain yourself some more."

Dan went on, amused by the excitement he had created: "You want to get some real information about the city administration. Well, it's impossible to start at the top. Start at the middle, or the bottom just to be sure. If you can bring a magistrate to trial on the grounds of his having been on familiar terms with a known underworld figure, you'll start something that'll be hard to stop. Is that clear to you, Colonel?"

"You mean—if that accusation can be substantiated, it will inevitably lead to the men higher up?"

Dan nodded. De Angelis, more practical than the Colonel, rapped: "How do you know this?"

"I know it," insisted Dan, "but I can't prove it. Now that leads to something else. You'll have to find a way to prove it, if you decide to use it."

"Where did you get the information?"

Dan considered for a few seconds. "Pasquale's name is one of several important ones on the list that was missing from Rosenberg's safe when they opened it. I know that, but I can't tell you how. Nobody knows where that damned list is, because we know Brand hasn't got it."

"It should be in the possession of the Federal District Attorney, should it not?" The Representative started thinking out loud. "He may decide to use it himself next year."

"He would, if he had it," Dan explained further, "use it when he starts running for Governor a year or so from now."

"Ian Brand for Governor?" The Colonel was surprised again.

Dan shrugged. "We figure it that way." To De Angelis: "But Brand hasn't got it. That's sure."

"But you're certain Pasquale's name is on that list?"

"I'm as sure as I can be without having seen it there myself. But there are more angles to this yet—" Dan continued earnestly. "You've got to promise me you'll get that information from somebody else before you use it. It would lead straight back to me and—"

"But we are paying you for that purpose. Mr. Fitzhugh!"

Dan spoke sharply: "You're paying me to give you information, not to get killed. Dead, I'm no good to you. Confirm that dope some place, and then you can use it. But don't use it till you have to."

De Angelis got up, walked to a window and did some heavy thinking. Then he turned and strode swiftly back to the desk. "I'll do my best. How's that? Colonel, you can consider me in the race."

Dan laughed to himself. They were like kids sworn to play-piracy as they shook hands. He got up to go. "Announce your ticket in August. You'll have Harding to run against. Tully's announcing the ticket."

He left them conferring. Once in the street he strolled up to Broadway, stared up at Trinity spire, turning purple against the evening sky, and started up Broadway.

He had given them a lighted fuse, and that's what they wanted. It would lead straight to Harding, he knew that. But he regretted a little that he had given it without further proof. But what the hell? Had to get started somewhere. The main thing now was to see that that list got to somebody who could give De Angelis a peek at it. Tough job, that.

Surer than fate, that was the thing that would nail Harding. Dan could imagine the row—and felt an unexpected twinge of vertigo at the thought that a city's chief executive could be so easily toppled from his throne. On the heels of that came to him a vivid thought of Billy Harding who wasn't, after all, such a bad guy. Forget that he was soft, and had done Dan a trick or two, he wasn't such a bad guy. On an impulse Dan hailed a cab and gave the Mayor's address in Chelsea Park. He grinned wryly to himself at his wild idea— but maybe he could drop a hint into Billy's brain that would put him wise. Never too late to mend ways. Dan admitted to himself he would much rather doublecross Portis than Billy—under some circumstances.

The cab pulled up before the house. He went in, was readily admitted, and in a few seconds, found himself in the living suite on the third floor.

"Mr. Fitzhugh," said a manservant into the bedroom.

"Come in, Dan!" a cheery voice called. Dan entered. Harding was twisting and craning before a pier glass, getting a wing collar fastened on a collar button.

"Let me help you." Dan pushed him back, shoved up his reddened face, and snapped the collar on. "There y'are!"

"These damn' things!" Harding stretched his neck. Then grinned. "What the hell, Danny! What's on your mind?"

The visitor sat down in an arm chair and started smoking. The Mayor tied his black tie and struggled into a tight-fitting white dress vest.

"Not a thing, Billy. I'm going by and I says to myself I'll say 'Hi' to the Mayor. Thought you'd be out with Helen by now."

"Hell, wish I was! I'm going to some banquet—Sons of How-Have-You-Been in honor of the Daughters of I-Wish-I-Was. You know those things."

"Only by hearsay. Why don't you cut 'em out?"

Harding, in progress of sliding into his Tuxedo jacket, looked at him. "Why? They keep me popular with people. Besides, they usually have pretty good drinks, somewhere in a room. That reminds me—Hey, Bozo!"

The manservant popped in.

"Couple cocktails, Bozo." Harding returned his attention to Dan. "Yes. Besides, in a way, I like 'em."

Dan spoke slowly, more seriously: "I should think more time in City Hall would do the trick just as well." For a moment Dan believed it himself.

Harding, straightening his tie in the mirror, laughed. "You sound like a newspaper. What for, spend my time in City Hall? The boys know their jobs. Everything is swell."

The cocktails came, and each had one.

Dan answered: "It is now, but—"

"Well, I'm popular, am I not? Say, did you hear of the gag I pulled the other night, introducing my executive secretary Aspinwall at a banquet? I said: 'Meet Clem Aspinwall. He's the day Mayor of New York, and I'm the nightmare.' I had 'em rolling in the aisles. This city eats up that sort of thing."

Dan was aghast. He considered Harding's quip to have been rotten politics, the kind of cheapness that had made Jim White so sore at him. But he only muttered:

"Broadway eats it up, you mean."

"What's the matter with you?" The youngish face of the executive regarded him with mock concern. "You sick?"

Dan forced a grin. "No. I'm just thinking that maybe things won't always go so well. A word to the wise ought to be—"

The Mayor downed the rest of the cocktail and poured out two more. "Stop groaning. You've got the vapors. Why should things change? Everything is for the best in this best of all worlds, or something like that. Even if I have to go to a banquet. Besides, there's a hot brawl on tonight at Julius Moses'. Wanta come up? Helen can get you somebody."

"No, thanks." Dan changed over inside. He couldn't get the man to listen. "I get my own women. Think I'll go to bed early tonight."

"You better, and when you feel like talking about the gayer things of life, come back." Harding whistled. Dan wondered if Harding's name was really on the Rosenberg list. He'd had no further inkling since the night Lila had told him about it. That reminded him of her warning about Helen. "You oughtn't to booze so much, Billy."

"Yes, Uncle!" Harding roared with laughter at him. Dan gave it up, an inexplicable feeling of helpless rage and disgust sweeping over him. The man was no man, but a child, the figure-head for smarter men. He got up and they started downstairs. On the second landing, Harding said hesitantly:

"Oh, say—you in a terrible hurry?"

"What's up?" They were by the door to the library.

Harding was embarrassed. "I wouldn't ask you to do this, only Albert's out some place, and—"

"Out with it!"

"Well, I've got to be on the City Hall steps to-morrow around twelve for some pictures, welcoming some women's committee from Chicago, and I want Bella there."

"Want me to tell her?" Dan's voice was cold.

Harding looked away, then back. "Tell her—yes. But will you give her something for me?"

"Sure. What is it?" Dan was growing irritated. They were just standing there.

Harding went into the library and snapped on the desk lamp. He sat down, drew a check book out of his desk, and started writing rapidly. Then he explained: "I wish you'd take this over to her. It's her allowance, and I don't like to put it in the mail. There!" He put the check in an envelope and handed it to Dan with a frank smile. Dan put it in his pocket.

Harding was driven away in his car. Dan took a cab uptown to the Cress Arms, an apartment hotel in West Seventy-first Street where Mrs. Harding lived. He announced himself over the house phone. Her voice irritably said: "Come on up, then."

She admitted him herself and he had no occasion to change his previous opinion of or liking for her. She had on, of all things, a mauve negligee that showed all he wanted to see of her plump neck showing fat lines, her bosom acreage and her short round arms. She had a pleasant face, with bitter lines around the eyes. Bella Harding had learned, by whatever means repugnant and humiliating to herself, to make the best of things. She didn't ask him to take a seat.

Dan remarked: "Billy asked me to give you your allowance check."

He pulled the envelope with the check out of his pocket, and she seized it, ripped it open and unfolded the check. Then she sighed. "Good, it's for a thousand. I needed it." Then she looked at him queerly. "Allowance? Is that what he told you?"

He nodded and started to deliver the rest of the message, but she went on: "Tell him I'll be at City Hall tomorrow in time for the pictures, all right. He phoned about it."

Dan took a chance, to satisfy his own curiosity. "A check for a grand is big for photographs."

She was silent, but he could see on her good-natured face the resentment she felt. She turned and went to the escritoire by the window and put the check in a little drawer, then locked it. "It's the usual," she said in a low tone. Then she turned and forced a smile.

"Have a drink?"

"Thanks."

"Otto!" she called into the next room. A tall German-looking man walked in calmly. Dan knew of him. "Mr. —er—Fitzhugh, you know Mr. Plessing. He's here on business from Berlin."

The men exchanged offhand greetings. Mrs. Harding handed them each a drink. Nobody said anything, and Dan drank quickly and lit a cigarette. He wondered what business Plessing was in. Bella Harding tried to keep a conversation going:

"We're probably going to the theater tonight. Know any good shows?"

Plessing's harsh, heavy voice said: "I would like much to see a good musical comedy with lots of beautiful young girls." His eyes gleamed blue.

She shot a side glance at him. She wasn't beautiful, or young. Dan got up. "I think you'll find a good one, all right. Well, thanks. Got to be going."

They both got up with alacrity, and ushered him out.

"Tell Billy I'll be there all right. And thanks for bringing the check."

"That's all right. Good night."

He left the Mayor's wife with her Berlin boy friend to gloat over the price of a public appearance. He had dinner in a speakeasy and went to a movie.

CHAPTER VI

"A Gangster on the Bench!"

"—AND I submit that my record during the past four years will prove that the people of the City of New York will give their support to the Democratic Party. When you go to the polls on the sixth day of November, you will cast your votes for those men who have shown, beyond the shadow of all possible doubt, that they are the ones to serve you as public officials." Burst of applause.

"Cocktail, Dan?" Lila offered him over the bar. She had to speak loudly to drown the radio. He shook his head. Firenze got up and took one. Lila smiled at him in a way Dan didn't like.

"During the last four years, as Mayor of the people of this great city, I have let nothing stand in the way of fulfilling the sworn vows of my office. The Democratic administration has carried out its promises to the letter, and stands side by side with a record of which it may well be proud!"

A newcomer walked in. Plunkett Doyle, the Hall's district leader of the midtown section. He was a large, compactly-built business man type, with short, brown, crinkly hair over a round face. He nodded to them all, not speaking but giving his attention at once to the voice of William T. Harding coming to them over the air. Then he accepted a drink, said something to Lila in a low voice, and sat down beside Dan. After a moment he said:

"I don't see any point in listening to this. He's not saying anything."

Firenze said nothing, but looked at Doyle. Lila shrugged. Dan knew that De Angelis was making a speech at the same time, but he didn't want to suggest tuning Billy off and the Italian in. He hoped somebody else would.

"And I further submit to you—"

Lila made a face. "He uses that word an awful lot. What's it mean?"

"What?"

"Submit."

"It means—er—submit."

Doyle laughed. Dan moved. Then the district leader nudged him, and jerked his head in the direction of the opposite room. As they went out two more men walked in: Ritchie and Blavitz, Assistant District Attorneys with Dan. He nodded to them. They sat down, and he went into the next room, deserted, with Doyle.

The local head man began: "Say, I wanted to ask you, Dan, if you had any dope."

"Ask me."

The crinkly-headed man talked in a low voice: "Here's the point: I got orders to put on extra steam to get out the vote. What I wanta know, is that just campaign hooey? Or are they really scared of De Angelis?"

"How d'you expect me to know?" Dan put down his empty glass, regretting he had come here, to this noisy joint, to listen in on the campaign speeches—it was late in September—instead of staying in his own room and getting De Angelis. He listened to Doyle:

"I figure it this way: this bird De Angelis hasn't got much drag with the public."

"Wrong, Plunkie. He's got more than you think, but he'll never be elected."

The man's brow cleared. "Then you don't think I gotta take 'em too seriously?"

Dan looked into the barroom, where the voice went on, and everybody listened, staring vacantly. "How do I know? Better take your orders where they come from."

"Yeah, I know, but you pick up a lot of inside stuff I never hear about. They leave me over there to make those votes come out."

"Well, De Angelis got nominated easy enough, didn't he?" Dan pointed out. "We know he's got personal backing of some kind, but nobody's sure." He was one of few to know that Portis, unofficially, had spent a lot of money on putting the Italian representative over in the Republican primaries. "So maybe he's more dangerous than anybody thinks."

The big man looked puzzled. "My own private idea is that they got a chance."

Dan laughed. "Not a prayer. Better get out the vote, boy. Six weeks you've got."

Doyle started to say something, but Lila came in. "What are you two whispering about in here? Come on in and be sociable."

"I don't want to listen to that bird talk," Doyle complained. "I heard it all before."

Lila laughed, looking at Dan. Her black evening dress made her look very alluring. "It's almost over. In ten minutes he'll be here. The station's only around the corner."

They went into the bar, and noisy conversation started up. Strangers began arriving, and Lila in a few minutes vanished upstairs. Dan saw her say something to Firenze as she left. Firenze walked over to Dan.

"Lila says we should all come up when Billy gets here."

"Brawl?"

The Italian nodded, and wet his lips. Dan wanted to smack him. "Billy's bringing Tobin and some girls from the show."

"Helen's show?"

The little swarthy man nodded. "Some swell girls. Tobin's a good skate."

"Yeah. How's Helen making out?"

"Oh, she's got a good part. Why not?" The man grinned slyly.

"When's it open?"

"Goes to Boston, Billy said, in a few weeks. They just started, ya know."

Dan nodded. He didn't know. But maybe the party would be good. He wished he had the nerve to listen to De Angelis. He fidgeted.

"Whatsa matter, Dan? Nervous?" The Italian watched him.

Ritchie came up, cocktail glass in hand. "Have a couple with me, laddies." His young face belied his keen mind. Dan knew the upper men had their eyes on the young Scotch lawyer. He was getting an edge deliberately ahead of the party—a sort of exclusive blowout for the younger men.

They began drinking and by the time Harding arrived a few minutes later, accompanied by a small man with enormous horn-rimmed glasses, they were feeling much better. Ritchie and Firenze were laughing loudly, but Dan, feeling inside him a peculiar suspense, was not so affected. He nursed an irritated mood and hoped he'd have a chance to sock the Italian secretary. Harding's arrival split them up and they went upstairs.

Harding had his arm, chummily, around the producer's shoulder. "How's the show look, Ben?"

"Oh, fine, Mr. Harding, fine! I think it'll be very good."

"Great! When can I come to rehearsals? I don't want this opera to be a flop." Harding sounded to Dan like an agent.

Tobin laughed obsequiously: "Oh, it won't be! You come round any time with Helen and you'll see."

Once inside Lila's upstairs apartment, Harding dragged Tobin off into a corner. Dan caught: "Give me an idea of the whole thing. Who's staging the dances?"

Their voices became a low, excited mutter in one corner. Doyle went over. "What's new, Mr. Harding? I wanted to ask if you thought that the campaign's going all right?"

Harding looked at his serious, anxious face—Doyle was too serious for most of them—then laughed. "Can't you see I'm busy with something important? I don't want to hear about the campaign. Go 'way." He laughed again. Tobin smiled anxiously. Dan turned away as the door opened and a crowd of girls came in, headed by Helen.

She screamed: "My baby boy! How's um speech-making?" She rushed across the room and threw her arms around the Mayor.

"Hello, kid! Great! Ben's telling me about the show. He tells me you're lousy."

She made a cute face, then flounced off: "Well, if I am, it's because I keep late hours—!" Tobin smiled, looking at Harding.

The Mayor got up and devoted himself to a wholesale introducing of girls to men. There were four girls in all to distribute between Dan, Ritchie, Blavitz, the young Jewish Assistant D.A. and Doyle. Dan stayed away from Lila, because Firenze was by her side the whole time. Now and again she threw companionable smiles at Dan. He stared back, resenting the wop.

Ritchie was among the girls. "Come on, step up, name y'r poison." One of them laughed. Another took a glass and sat down apart from the rest. Dan sat down beside her.

"Don't you go for this kind of a racket?"

Her big blue-gray eyes looked at him softly. Dan was women's meat. "Certainly," she smiled. "Only we just came from a rehearsal, and—"

"Yeah. Well, stoke up and forget it."

Harding joined them. "Found a pal, Danny? That's great."

"I thought I was doing all right." Dan looked down sideways at the girl's well-shaped legs. Her good figure wasn't concealed by a tight-fitting red French flannel dress. He liked her.

Harding: "This little girl, Danny, is one of the greatest little hot hoofers I've ever seen. Wait'll you see her when the show opens."

"You know all about it, don't you, Billy?" Dan prodded.

Harding waved a hand and straightened up. "Say, it's going to be a great opera. You know, a lot of people think I ought to've been an actor."

"You are," Dan laughed.

Helen cut short Harding's retort. "Say, let's go some place and dance. I don't wanta hang around here and get stinko."

"Not this chicken," Billy told her. "I'm not going to get plastered tonight. Baby, this campaign's tough. You don't know."

Helen appealed to Dan: "Aw, tell him he doesn't treat me right. What do I care if he has to make speeches? I'm workin' hard too and I wanna have a good time!"

"Maybe you better take her hoofing, Billy," Dan suggested. "What about you?" he turned to the blue-gray-eyed girl next to him.

"I'd rather not," she said and kept her eyes on Dan. He smiled at her.

Harding turned back to Helen: "See what she says? There's a girl with sense."

Helen pouted. Harding slapped her suddenly on the back. She slapped him back and then they fell in each other's arms, laughing. That left Dan with the blue-gray-eyed girl. They talked and he found she came from California, did a specialty in the show and her name was Betty de la Roche.

Dan looked across the room and saw Lila alone. Firenze was talking to Ritchie. Everybody was getting noisier as more drinks were passed. Dan helped himself to another and excused himself from Betty. He crossed

to Lila. Blavitz yelled at him: "Hi, you old crook!"
Dan pushed him playfully. Lila said nothing when he
sat down beside her.

"What's the matter with you tonight?"

She shook her head.

"Like the wop now better?"

"Maybe."

"Maybe little Albert will say nice things to the
Mayor and you won't have any raids."

"Maybe."

"Hey, what the hell——"

She burst out: "You've got a hell of a nerve promot-
ing some other dame under my nose and in my own
place."

"What do you want me to do when the wop is right
on your neck?"

"He's not!"

"The hell he's not. Besides, she's cute."

"Oh, leave the kid alone!"

Helen charged into them suddenly, with more than
one drink in her already. "Wheee—Billy's comin' to
rehearsal tomorrow. Hear that, girls?"

Ritchie bawled: "We'll all be there!" Doyle roared:
"Me, too, Billy!"

Billy stood up and struck an attitude: "As Mayor
of the People of the city of New York, I invite you to
rehearsal tomorrow."

Tobin said in a quiet voice: "You're all welcome."

"Good ole Benny!" Helen shrieked. "And if I'm a little late tomorrow, you won't fire me?"

The producer looked at Harding. "You can be as late as you like."

Lila said in Dan's ear: "How about the campaign?"

"What's he care?" Dan was looking at Betty across the room. Firenze spotted Dan next to Lila and walked over to them. Dan said to him: "Why don't you get him the hell home to bed? He's gotta make a speech tomorrow noon."

The Italian sneered. "He can take care of himself."

Dan got sore. "You know damn' well Tully doesn't care for this business—not during campaigning. The idea is to get elected."

"You keep your advice to yourself! He can handle himself without help from a shyster!" Little Albert gazed down at Dan steadily, hostilely.

Dan made to stand up, saying: "Also he's going along without help from his secretary." He smiled at the Italian.

Lila's hand was on his arm and her voice was cold. "Two little boys fighting again. Sit down!"

Dan relaxed. Harding and Helen, on a round of the room arm in arm, were on them. Harding, despite the drinks, sensed the tension. "Whatsa matter?"

Lila laughed: "They're fighting over the fair white body, Billy. I'm flattered."

Helen: "I wish somebody'd fight over mine."

Harding: "Aw, baby, I won't let 'em!"

"My hero!" Then they caromed away. Firenze went over for another drink.

Lila said to Dan: "You're getting to be a crusader."

"Like hell. But I never saw such a collection of idiots. You know me. I like my fun, so why shouldn't anybody else? But there's a time for that, and a time for other things. This is a time for sense."

Lila's eyes burned. "Something's wrong with you? Love, liquor or stomach trouble?"

"Stomach trouble, baby, but not literally." He smiled without expression and caressed her cheek with his hand. She didn't move.

"You're a killer, all right. You ought to go and get a headache powder."

He looked over at Betty de la Roche across the room, now entertaining Blavitz. Their eyes met. Dan turned back to Lila. "I will—again not literally." The hostess' eyes flamed.

"I'll tell you frankly, big boy, you burn me up. I wish to God you'd either stay in one spot, or keep out of here."

"Then don't mix me up with the wop. I'm fussy."

"I'll mix you, or anybody else—that's what comes of being talkative!"

He leaned closer to her and put his hand on her thigh. He meant what he said: "You'll tell me lots more things."

"You're a bastard."

He grinned and nodded. "But look what fun I have."

She stared at him, something near hate twisting her mouth. "I mix you and the wop because you—you—"

"Then don't do it. Because I mean what I say enough times to be listened to when I talk." He paused and laughed. His own vague nervousness and irritation was losing him his sense of proportion. "Listen to me making speeches."

She made an inarticulate sound and looked away. Dan saw Harding, surrounded by Tobin, obsequious; Doyle, would-be jovial; and a couple of girls, including Helen on his neck as always. Dan dropped: "The friends of the Mayor."

"Oh, they'll take care of him! Don't forget there're more friends than those."

"The friends of the Mayor will see him in hell."

"Oh, cut it out! . . . Albert!" The wop came over. "Albert, tell this guy to go away."

The two men looked at each other. Dan said, low, to Lila: "I told you." He got up and left them without a word, bored suddenly. He rejoined Betty, and said to Blavitz:

"Leo, go 'way. This is my friend." She smiled at him.

The young Jewish attorney protested volubly: "Aw, gimme a break, Dan! Ya want all the beauties in the place? Just like a goddam Irishman."

Dan took him by the shoulders and spun him round to face the Harding group, now singing as Ritchie played inaccurately on the baby upright piano in one corner. "There's somebody for you, Leo. Goom-bye, please." And he shoved him. Leo went, leering back over his shoulder. Dan said down at the girl:

"What say we leave this?"

She nodded. Her big eyes were wide. He shot a glance at his wrist-watch. "Near one. Let's go."

She stood up and they started for the door. Dan didn't think anybody saw them leaving, till Harding's voice cried: "Hi, wait a minute, Dan. I'm going too."

But a chorus of voices drowned him, white arms around his neck smothered him. Dan walked out, then noticed Lila's and the Italian secretary's eyes on him. He waved a hand and shut the door.

It turned out Betty had an apartment, so they bought food and drink and went there. After the first gin and ginger ale, Dan went to the phone and called the desk: "Will you send a boy out for all the morning papers he can get?"

In a few minutes a bellhop came with six papers.

Betty squatted beside him on the small divan. He patted her leg. "I want to see what happened."

The first headlines hit him:

" 'A GANGSTER ON THE BENCH!' SAYS DE ANGELIS."

The other papers carried the same thing. The story, including highlight quotations from De Angelis' speech before the People's Franchise Union—to which Dan had wanted to listen—told how De Angelis called Magistrate Antonio Pasquale a gangster and accused him of outright and shameless dealings with the underworld. One sentence read:

"It is an outrage to American justice and to the honest citizens of our great city that a Magistrate should be in the debt of the underworld. This is but an example of an administration which will leave in history a record of unparalleled corruption."

Dan read every paper, while Betty fidgeted. He told her: "This will raise hell."

"Won't Mayor Harding be worried?"

He threw the papers on the floor and kissed her. "No, I don't think he will."

"Oh, then there's nothing to worry about!"

"No. I doubt if Mayor Harding will take that, or anything else, very seriously."

"Have another drink. I'll fix it for you." The girl got up.

Dan smoked and watched her and thought. She was a nice kid and tomorrow was time enough to worry.

But had De Angelis confirmed that fact? Or had he gone ahead on Dan's tip-off? There was dynamite on the premises, with plenty of angles to figure out. One: had that list turned up? Two: where had it been, or where was it now? Three: was anybody going to pin it on Dan? That much clear, Dan put it all out of his mind until the morning.

CHAPTER VII

Billy Picks the Goats

THINGS happened fast after that, and Dan was just catching his breath. Because the newspapers and the reform element took De Angelis seriously, and Pasquale got scared and admitted to having been a borrower from the deceased Rosenberg. That caused a rumpus, which left Dan sitting on tacks, since so far as he could learn nobody had located the list and De Angelis had taken a chance. That it wasn't as long a chance as Dan had thought was proven by Pasquale's panicky confession. The Magistrate claimed to have borrowed the money indirectly through a prominent man since dead.

Lila had called him the morning he got to his office, after leaving Betty's apartment. Her voice was throaty with fear:

"Dan, did you read the papers?"

"Of course."

"Well—?"

"Well nothing. That's all there is to it."

She was silent, and he could feel coming over the wire the tangible quality of her apprehension and curiosity.

She wanted to know if he had spilled the dope to any one, or if not, did he think she had, despite his threat, talked to some one else? He said nothing, and let her stew. He didn't go near her for weeks, and now it was early in October. She called him up four times, and he managed to be out.

Then he had seen Portis, who shook him by the hand cordially.

"I believe you were right, Mr. Fitzhugh. We have started something."

"Tell me, Colonel, did De Angelis confirm somehow the facts about Pasquale, or did he go ahead on what I told him?"

The Colonel ruminated, frowning. "He consulted no one about that speech. I don't know."

"Anyway, tell him I expected him to keep his promise."

"Oh, I am certain that he is an honorable man. At all events, we are all very jubilant."

"Don't be. He won't be elected."

The financier's face fell. "You still think that?"

Dan nodded. "You wanted to start something, even if you couldn't elect a Fusion Mayor, and take my word for it, this will lead you where you want it to."

They shook hands. Dan hadn't seen him since, having spent most of his time deliberately cultivating the candidate for District Attorney—Judge Edward Quinn, ex-State Supreme Court Justice and a good organization man. The dear old gentleman was baffled by the Pasquale business, and the master minds wanted to know how De Angelis had found out about it. They concluded somebody other than Brand had shown the list to the Fusion candidate. Obviously, they couldn't have guessed that Harding had spilled it to Helen Faire, starting the chain to Dan. Harding had a scared look at the brain session the night after the De Angelis speech. The upshot of that meeting was Harding's pronouncement in response to the horrified outcry of the press and public opinion:

"It is not within my executive powers to remove Magistrate Pasquale. I am sure that he is innocent, but will hesitate in no wise in the performance of my duty to the people of the City of New York."

But it hadn't stopped there, as Dan had known it wouldn't. The Republicans in the State Legislature, sensing a good chance to pin something on the Hall, threatened a public inquiry. The day after that, Governor Van Brunt Adams refused to act in the matter, saying that the city was possessed of the proper machinery to settle the question, and consequently he had not the right to interfere. There it rested, because the campaign was on and everybody, even the Republican press, agreed that the investigation of Magistrate Pasquale's connection with the criminal world should not be confused by electioneering animus.

However, full steam was up, and a heavy Democratic

vote was going to be cast. No doubt of that, because the dereliction of one public officer meant nothing to anybody—not yet. So Dan cultivated Judge Quinn in order to keep his own job under the next administration. One night, he and Ritchie and Blavitz were called in by Calloway. The latter told them:

"Judge Quinn will undoubtedly be elected. He is a fine man and will make an honest public prosecutor. However, he has never before come in such direct contact as he will come with the New York City criminal courts. It will be up to you, gentlemen, to pilot him through the mazes and to help him, by your experience, to avoid many pitfalls."

All three Assistant D.A.'s looked at him, and all knew that they would retain their jobs—to see that Judge Quinn kept his hands off where they should stay off. In simplest words, they all knew that Quinn was too innocent a soul to be one of the boys, and it would be better if he didn't know everything.

Nevertheless, Dan cultivated him. He rode around with him nights on campaign speech tours. He piloted him through the labyrinth of the city organization and clubs, and built up personal contacts. He pitched in and wrote an occasional address for him, which the Judge delivered with unction from the manuscript. It all helped, and Quinn was grateful.

This night early in October, the election a month away and the famous De Angelis speech nearly a

month behind, Dan brought Quinn and the pretty
young secretary they carried around to the District
Club run by Plunkett Doyle. Everywhere they had
been the hand of Honest Tom was felt, capped by
Harding's speech four days before, in which he had
said:

"I will carry out to the letter the campaign pledges
of my party and my organization, of which Thomas
Tully is the leader."

Editorials came out and said Harding was nothing
but a figure-head, which everybody who cared already
knew, and those who didn't know didn't care. All square
and hunky-dory. No longer was there a doubt in anybody's mind that Honest Tom was the strong man, and
Harding was his front. In a few places, there was talk of
building Harding up to take Jim White's place as
Democratic head in the eyes of the nation, but somehow, for no tangible reason, the plan never got very
far.

On the second floor of the Club, Doyle was harangu-
ing his members, consisting of rows and rows of nondescript men, largely men in business with small salaries
and big families, and including also a fair number of
women politicians. Dan and Quinn and the secretary,
Nan Selden, stopped and listened.

Doyle spouted: "I don't like the way you boys and
girls are covering the district. You've got to knuckle
down and work. Don't think you were through when

you got 'em out for the primaries. It's up to you now to see that they register. And every Democrat who registers must vote on Election Day, if he has to be dragged to the polls. Here I am, slaving for you, working hard, attending to your contracts, and you sit around and stare at me! I won't have it!"

He shook a finger at their docile faces. "And let me tell you this: Any member who lays down on the job won't have any contract put through for him for a year! I mean that!" The red-faced man glared ferociously, and they were thoroughly intimidated. That threat was serious, contracts being little favors—such as promotions for city servants, fixing speed tickets, and a million odd little things that a political club can do for its rank and file.

Doyle smiled and changed the subject, looking over the heads of his audience at Quinn and Dan. He continued: "Now, tonight I've got a special treat for you. Judge Quinn, Democratic candidate in the coming election for District Attorney, is here himself tonight to tell you a few things of interest to you all. Judge Edward Quinn!"

Hands clapped, heads craned, and Quinn made his way down the rough aisle to the front of the room. Dan took the girl's hand and they went downstairs to Doyle's private office.

"Let's get this speech done, Nan. What'll it be about?" He shed his hat and overcoat and sat at the desk. The girl, a blonde, blue-eyed and trim in feature and body, did likewise. She got out her notebook, and sat opposite to him, expectantly.

"I don't know, Mr. Fitzhugh——"

"Dan," he suggested.

"I don't know what the speech should be about. Haven't you talked with Judge Quinn?" She stared at him seriously.

"No, I haven't. Not necessary. Well, let's see——" He leaned back in the chair and gazed at the ceiling. Quinn had to talk at the meeting of the Manhattan Women Voters' Club the next day, and the dames had to be handed some pap.

"Let's start this way: Ladies—there won't be any gentlemen there—ladies, I am come before you in a new rôle—that of candidate for an office which vitally affects every one of you and your children and husbands. We better get in something about homes and that hooey, like this: It is my avowed task to serve you, as public prosecutor, in that way which the mandate of the people shall dictate. I am not your enemy, but your protector. It is my duty to guard zealously the rights of the citizen and of the home—to permit nothing to interfere with the orderly progress of the lives of those who are most important in our community. Paragraph or pause.

"That's not a bad start, baby. Now let's see. We

ought to put some guts into it. These women voters are demons. Well, let's rest a minute whilst I think."

Nan leaned back. "Don't you think this is all very interesting, Mr. Fitzhugh?"

"Dan."

She smiled and actually blushed. "D-Dan."

"That's better. Your first job of the kind, eh?" He liked her hair peeping out from under her blue cloche hat, and the way the whiteness of her neck contrasted with the dark blue of her dress. Her hands were white and strong looking.

She looked at him and away again continuously, as she talked.

"I've been with Judge Quinn for two years, but I never had anything like this. You know what I mean?"

"Sure. Sitting around dumps like this. If it's new to you, it doesn't make much difference."

"Oh—I—I like it all right! I've met such a lot of interesting people, and I—" She stopped, confused, again.

Dan realized she was much more charming, had more on the ball, than he had thought at first. "You're very pretty," he told her.

She smiled, pleased. Her voice was low when she said: "Hadn't we better get back to the speech?"

"Yeah. What'd I say last? Never mind. We have to have something good come now. These women—"

"Don't you think the women are important in this election?"

He laughed. "They can be fooled like anybody else." He leaned back and stared at the ceiling some more. He murmured: "What the hell can we say? Promise 'em service and protection? Hooey! Talk about Pasquale? No. Indictments, rackets, criminal procedure? More hooey! Well—"

"How about civic trust? I've heard the Judge use that frequently in his own speeches."

Dan was suddenly disgusted. "It's all lousy! We got to put some teeth in this thing, either now or damn' soon." He thought long and hard. He bore in mind that Jessup, not being renominated, could be a goat, was one already in fact, though nothing as yet had been heaped on him. Then he brought his feet down off the desk with a bang. He grabbed the girl's arm.

"Run up and see if he's finished gassing, will you? Tell him I've got an idea. Quick, sweetheart."

Commendably, she got up and left the room quickly. Dan arose and walked around, revolving his idea. In a minute Nan returned.

"He'll be down in a minute. He's shaking hands."

"Okay, sweet. I'll buy you a dinner next week. Now you better toddle home."

She looked doubtful. "Judge Quinn told me to stay."

"Never mind that. We won't need you any more

tonight. Skedaddle like a darling and have dinner with me Tuesday."

She considered, inspected him, then nodded brightly and went to don her coat. "All right."

"Phone me at the office. I'll see you before then anyway."

"Good night."

"By-by, sweet." Then he forgot her.

He had had about two minutes to himself when Quinn came in. He was old—too old, Dan thought, to be D.A. 'Way over sixty, with a fair record as State Supreme Court Justice behind him. Kindly eyes looked out of a gentle old gray face. Thin gray hair covered sparsely a small round head, and his voice was soft but clear.

Dan shoved a chair around for him and drew the blinds down on the windows which fronted on the street.

"This is hard work for an old man, Mr. Fitzhugh." He sat down and began the labor of lighting a panetela.

Dan leaned over the table toward him and began talking: "I've got an idea, Judge, that I think is good for your speech tomorrow. I sent the girl home, but if you like I'll get it in shape in plenty of time."

The old gray face was turned to him in an attitude of judicial, slightly vague, listening. Dan doubted if the man would really grasp the idea. Anyway—

"We've got to put some teeth into your campaign, because just to talk about duty, trust, and all that, gets dull."

"But they are promises," the veteran protested.

Dan ignored that. "Here we are, now. The Rosenberg case and the Carmody trial are getting a lot of attention. We know they're announcing the Carmody trial date tomorrow, for November 12th, because the papers have been squawking. Now, we're sure the Carmody trial is nothing. He won't be convicted."

Quinn nodded. He knew that much of the inside. Dan felt encouraged. If this went over, it put him right with the old man, and that meant something. "Now, you promise the public that if Carmody is not convicted—imply, however, he's the real murderer—you will bring the murderer of Al Rosenberg to justice within a month of taking office!"

"Oh, Good Lord, how can I do that?" The Judge was startled.

Dan returned to the wars. "Easy as pie. Jessup can't convict Carmody. I know that. There's not even a good circumstantial case against the mugg. Jessup doesn't care, because he's through anyway. When you do take office, you make a big thing of examining the records of the case, then throw up your hands in despair. Jessup gummed it up so it's impossible to do anything."

The idea was good and Dan knew it. But the Judge protested:

"It's not exactly fair. I don't like to—"

"It's damn' good politics," Dan urged.

The old gentleman thought in silence. Then his face brightened. Dan could see that he had managed to square it up in his own mind. He nodded with unexpected enthusiasm. "You're right, Mr. Fitzhugh. The Rosenberg case *is* in the public eye, and that will make a very good campaign plank. I wish I had thought of it before."

"Fine. Now I'll get to work on the speech myself."

"Wait a minute." The Judge considered some more. "This is really a daring thing to do. I'd like to get Mayor Harding's approval before we go ahead."

Dan almost said: "You're crazy. Tully's the man." But he didn't, and in a few minutes, at Quinn's insistence, they were off to a midtown hotel, where Dan learned Harding was expecting Quinn anyway.

Inside of ten minutes, driven by Quinn's chauffeur in the campaign tour car, they were landed at the hotel. Harding kept a suite here steadily, and Dan had been on some parties in it. As they crossed the lobby to the elevator, Dan looked at his watch. Close to twelve. They went to the suite.

Harding, in a silken bathrobe, black pajamas underneath, let them in.

They shook hands. "Good evening, Judge! Come in, Dan."

They sat down. Harding looked tired, and seemed

to be forcing an air of cordiality with impatience. Dan looked around the room, last looking at the bedroom door, which was open about two inches. Quinn had his back to it.

"Mr. Harding, I want to explain something to you —a new idea I've had for my campaign, and before injecting the point into my speech tomorrow, I felt it better to discuss it with you." Thenceforward, his dull, gentle voice explained the whole thing as if it were his own. Dan was credited only with having contributed some minor points. Dan looked at the ceiling. Harding listened.

Dan marveled at Quinn's naïveté and looked blankly at Billy.

Finally the old man was finished, and Harding sat still.

"Do you think it a good idea?"

Harding got up for a cigarette and laughed. "Sure, it's a great idea! It doesn't hurt anybody, even yourself. What can you lose?"

Dan's eyes wandered again to the bedroom door. Harding went on:

"We've got to have goats in politics. Crandall was one, and now I think it's damn funny if we make Jessup another." The comicality of it struck him suddenly and he laughed. "Goats! Boy, you gotta have 'em. Go to it, Judge, ole boy!"

Quinn looked slightly pained at the familiarity, but

seemed pleased despite it. "Oh, another thing! Mr.
Fitzhugh has been very helpful to me so far, and if
elected, I want your tacit approval to keeping him in
office with me."

Billy grinned at Dan. "Why, sure! I think that's a
swell idea."

Quinn beamed on Dan, who said: "Thanks very
much."

The Assistant District Attorney happened then to
look past Quinn at the bedroom door. Through the
crack, he saw a female figure cross the room. One bare
shoulder, a strip of torso and half a white breast.
Pajamas, dark hair—Helen—Helen Faire.

CHAPTER VIII

Robbery, Slander and Sudden Death

OLLENDORFF had called Dan at his hotel, and the Big Noise's voice had sounded rattled. Dan said into the receiver:

"Be down right away."

He dressed fast, and taxied to Harding's Chelsea Park place. In the library he found Harding, Ollendorff and Dietrich. They all stared round-eyed. Dan let himself down in an easy chair and, reaching up with one hand, turned the standing lamp away so that the light did not fall on his face.

Ollendorff talked: "Dan, maybe you can help us on this. It looks like a job for the D.A.'s office."

"What's the matter with Jessup?" Dan asked, knowing perfectly well.

Harding looked uncomfortable. "You know, Dan, we didn't want to bother him with this. His term hasn't much longer to go, and—"

Dan nodded. That meant they wanted to keep this under cover, and Jessup, being one of the chosen goats, mightn't like it if they gave him more trouble than he had already. Dietrich, in his customary methodical manner, explained it with a touch of impatience:

"Dan, the situation is this. You know that the Rosenberg list we're so worried about has vanished. You knew that? Now, we have suspected that De Angelis saw it somewhere, or else someone who has seen it told him about it. Anyway, with only some two weeks—" it was October 19th—"to Election Day, we can't take any chances."

Dan said: "What can you do now that you couldn't do before? And where do I come in?"

The sachem raised a hand. "Wait a minute. Here's the point: we have learned where the list is!"

Dan jumped. "The hell you have!"

His first thought was one of relief. That would prevent any last-minute blow-up. His second was that maybe its contents had reached De Angelis and the blow-up was already under way. Dietrich smiled grimly:

"One of Frank's boys found out where it is. How was it, Frank?"

The boss of the Police swelled. One of his boys had done a neat bit of work. "Well, you know what I suspected when it was taken. All we had to do was check up on those that were in on it. I've had my boys working on that angle for some time now. Well, McCafferty learned that one of Brand's boys had a lot of money about a week after the killing and the opening of the safe. A little more careful check-up—I can show you a copy of McCafferty's report—and we find he sold something to Squire, editor of the *Press*."

Dan breathed carefully. Harding's eyes glistened, even if he *had* heard the tale a few minutes before. Dan wondered where he fitted in. There was something fishy about this. Well, he would out with it.

Ollendorff finished: "McCafferty checked up even more thoroughly and found out from a girl he knows who works on the paper that she has actually seen the list in Squire's office."

Dan scoffed: "Get out! Squire is a hard-boiled newspaper man. He's no God-damned fool. He's not leaving a thing like that around for some stenographer to see."

Ollendorff frowned. "I can't help how tough he is. The fact remains that he did once permit it to be seen. I don't exactly know how it happened, but it happened. The list is in Squire's hands."

"I don't believe it. He'd have printed it a long time ago."

"But he hasn't, for some reason," Dietrich put in. "There are other names on the list too. Park Avenue."

Dan wanted to play safe and cover himself from all angles. "I don't see why you draw me into this. It's up Jessup's alley, or better yet, Tom Tully's."

Harding protested in a near-panic. "Listen, for Christ's sake! I'm on that list as a borrower. We gotta get it back and I don't want Tully to know!"

Dan leaned back. Now he was putting his finger on the real situation. "Then what do you want me to do?" He had an idea in his head, but he wanted them to talk first. This looked too much like more goat-picking at the moment.

Dietrich calmed him. Dan could see they were all worried, more now than they'd ever been when they had had no suspicion of the whereabouts of the list. "The point is, Dan, we don't want to go to Tully, or to Jessup, nor, obviously, to Judge Quinn, for advice. What we want to know frankly is, have you any legal machinery you can employ to get that list away from Squire?"

Dan shook his head disgustedly. "Not without all the publicity in the world. Or without Tully and everybody finding out. That's too chancy. And if Brand got wise the D.A.'s office was trying to rustle papers that belong to him—wow!"

Harding sank back in his chair, biting his nails. "We got to do something."

Dan said: "I'll tell you what we'll—"

Firenze came into the room suddenly. He growled: "Sorry to butt in, but this is a nuisance." He had on hat and coat.

"What's the matter?" Harding's voice was querulous.

The Italian hesitated and looked around. "I'll have to explain it to you."

Harding jerked a hand. "The hell! Out with it. I got more important things to—"

"Well, she says for the lunch tomorrow, it bein' campaign time and all, she'll have ta have fifteen hundred instead of a grand."

Everybody else put on blank faces, as if they hadn't the vaguest idea what Firenze was talking about. Harding rapped: "That's a lousy, stinkin'—" Then he changed his mind. "Sit down a minute. She can wait."

"Yeah, but she said—" Firenze squawked.

"Sit down!" The wop sat, eyes gleaming angrily. He didn't like this business and Dan didn't blame him.

Dietrich took it up again: "You were saying, Dan?"

"I was saying—I'll get the list for you."

"What?"

"I said I'll get the list."

"How?" Harding sat forward, wetting his lips. "Careful how you use the office."

Dan waved a hand. "Hell with that! I'll go down now and get it from Squire."

Ollendorff blurted: "You're crazy!"

"Think so? Maybe I am." He leaned back as if giving up the idea. Dietrich complained:

"Frank, this is serious. If Dan can do it—Go ahead, Dan. What's your method?"

Dan explained with feigned laboriousness. "I know Squire. I worked for him once and I see his reporters about twice a week. He runs a morning tab, and that means he's there now. What time is it? Near twelve. Well, he has to stick around till about three or four. I can muscle in and take it."

"With all those men standing around? You can't hold 'em up!" Ollendorff protested.

Dan stood up. "Stop belly-aching! You want the list?" He inspected their eager, scared faces. "All right. I'll try to get it."

Dietrich stood up too. "We'll wait here for you. Now hustle, and come back alive."

Firenze said to Harding: "Gimme that check, Billy. I wanta get goin'. She squawks and—"

His mind on Dan, the Mayor made out a new check at his desk. He tore up the one the secretary gave back to him. Dan left them, and heard Firenze's steps coming down the steps after him. He didn't wait, but, after looking around to see that Firenze went the opposite way, walked downtown two blocks, then across, then took a trolley to the narrow street not far from Park Row where the *Morning Press* was put out in a square six-storied whitish building with large windows like a factory. From across the street he could hear the rumble of the presses running off the home edition.

He went in and up to the fifth floor where the city room was located. Typewriters banged, men in top-coats and felt hats lounged before clacking machines, industriously turning out the next day's news. Office boys, looking greenish in the strong artificial light, came and went. Many of the men nodded to Dan. He crossed to one of the older ones, a police reporter.

"H'lo, Sam. How's things?" They shook hands.

"Great, Danny. What the hell you doin' in this dump?" They lit cigarettes.

Dan grinned. "Public relations, me bye. I'm in the neighborhood, so I thought I'd come in and say hello to Jim."

The gray-headed reporter with a boozy look and the bored eyes of a man accustomed to long waits in the cold rooms of jails and courts, said: "His office's over there. Say, gimme some hot dope, will ya? What's the inside on Carmody?"

Dan looked around. "Oh, I dunno! Maybe he'll be convicted. If not, Quinn'll go back and get him."

The old man sneered. "Get out! That's hooey and you know it."

"Good reading, though. Jesus, what do you expect me to tell you? That Carmody's innocent?"

"Yeah. Tell me Stein did it."

Dan grinned and said: "Wait'll I see Jim a few minutes. I haven't seen the old coot in months. Stick around."

"Okay."

Dan wandered through aisles between barren desks, papers littering everything, typewriters standing with a neglected look among disordered scraps of copy paper, some bearing incompleted sentences, others fully typed. Yesterday's editions lay about, torn, trampled, everything thrown aside for the morrow. He came to the partitioned office in the corner. The door was open and a man, inside, yelled:

"Klamroth!"

A young man at a near-by desk got up and lounged in with Dan. Squire at his desk looked at Dan, nodded, then talked to the other man: "Get me a first from the press. Quick. And send Fearing up here. Page Two is lousy." The youth went out. "Hello, you lawyer. What's up?"

Dan shut the door behind him. He had three minutes. He inspected Squire, not unaware that his heart was pounding with healthy excitement. Through the flimsy partition came the clack of typewriters, and the walls transmitted throughout the entire building the rhythmic rumbling swish of the presses three floors below. Squire was a short, stocky man, powerfully built, but not necessarily very strong. His piercing eyes, backed by moral and mental courage, stared with casual cordiality, from under bushy eyebrows. He was a hard-boiled newspaperman, and a good one. The *Press* sold a million and more a day. Dan sat down:

"I was coming from a brawl over the way and stopped in to chin."

"Why not pick daytime? What's new? How's Billy and all the boys?"

"Great. We're going to win. Only for one thing."

"Yeah?" Squire was scanning the front page of another tabloid which got out before the *Press.* "What's that?"

"The Rosenberg list." Dan watched him and drew his feet up under his chair. He placed his right hand in his overcoat pocket as if reaching for a pack of cigarettes. Squire looked up at him, the casualness gone from his eyes. Dan added: "Give it to me."

Squire laughed in his face. "You crazy?"

"Not a bit. You've got it. Bought it from Brand's dick. I want it. What say?"

Squire's look changed. He seemed to undergo an inner convulsion. The steel in his mind was bracing. "I've got it to print. You and your crooked bosses can't stop this paper."

Dan stood up. "The hell we can't." He kept his voice low and even. He brought his clenched fist in his right hand coat pocket up, as if pointing a hidden revolver. Squire saw it, and paled. "That's a lot of hooey and you know it. I came down for the list, so come across."

"God damn you for a crook!" Squire began to seethe. "You're not fighting me, smart boy. You're up against a newspaper. I've got that list, and I'm going to print it if hell blows up under my feet. I wasn't going to, but now I will."

Dan grew impatient. Squire had more guts than he had thought. He spoke swiftly and intensely: "Listen.

I've got a revolver in my pocket. Give me the list or I'll let go. You don't want a bullet in your chest."

"That's murder."

"No. I can shoot enough to make it hurt. You haven't got the guts to hold out on me. Where's the list?"

Squire's face was yellow. He had the moral force of a crusader, but no physical courage. Not now. He reached toward a drawer, unlocked it and brought out a folder with shaking hands. Dan grabbed it. The man from the press room might be coming any second. It looked like the list. "If this isn't it, you'll get in trouble."

"You God-damn' stinking rat!" Squire almost wept. He was scared and mad at the same time. "I'll print the story of this hold-up in the next edition!"

Dan jeered: "Sure you will! You were held up within twenty-five feet of your own city room full of muggs. The hell you will."

The man's hands clenched and unclenched. His eyes blazed. His voice broke on the next words: "I'll print it—" and his eyes goggled when Dan brought an empty hand out of his pocket, at the same time stowing the list in a breast pocket. Dan backed to the door.

"This is my racket, Jim. You're not dealing with individuals, you're dealing with the machinery of Government." He felt the door pushed open against his back. The man from the press room. "Well, so long, Jim! Thanks for a pleasant visit. Be good!"

He turned and went out. He told the pressroom foreman: "Mr. Squire asked me to tell you to hold up the second for a new Page Two. Don't bother him now." The man hurried away, scowling. Dan closed the door, and walked back to where his friend was sitting.

"Come into the office tomorrow, Sam. Maybe I'll have something for you."

The man nodded. "Wanta drink?"

Dan shook his head and strolled out. Once in the street he hopped a cab, got out at Times Square, walked into a subway kiosk, came out another one, went into a drugstore, from that into a hotel lobby and out its north entrance. That brought him a block from his hotel. Safely he gained his room. There he drew the blinds, locked the door, ripped the cover off his portable typewriter, drew the list from his pocket and proceeded to make a swift copy. His fingers flew, and he didn't stop to reflect, consider or absorb the contents. His mind, attuned to the swift typing, concentrated on the accuracy of what it was doing. He would have time enough to think about this afterwards. The idea was to get back down to Chelsea Park. What he would do with the copy he would decide later. He finished in half an hour, slipped the copy in an envelope, covered the machine, lit a cigarette, and went downstairs. He asked the elevator boy to put the envelope in the safe for him. He watched while it was done.

Outside he picked up another cab and was driven

swiftly to the Mayor's house. When he entered the upstairs library, he had been gone a little more than an
hour and three quarters. The room was gray with
smoke. Firenze's eyes gleamed like a cat's from a dark
corner. He was back from his errand. Harding's vest
was open, his hair ruffled, his voice raw when he ar-
ticulated:

"Get it?"

"I got it."

Dietrich said nothing, but walked over and opened
a window. The cold air was like the relief they all felt.
Harding clutched the list. They all read it.

Exclamations came from them in volleys:

"Jesus, if they'd printed that! Good-by!"

"Looka that! There's plenty of hop-heads on Park
Avenue. What a guy!"

Sweat of relief at passing danger stood on Harding's brow. He said: "Danny, the city's yours. What
a break!"

Then they stopped talking, and sat in sudden lifeless silence. Dan felt triumphant. He even grinned
maliciously at the Italian secretary, who stared back,
expressionless.

In a few moments, Dan left them to talk. He had
done his share. He walked from the building, turned
uptown and started through to the avenue on a narrow, dark street. He heard a truck rumble into the
lower end of the block, back of him. He looked around.

It was coming fast. He swore. A bullet rang past him. He ducked. Another ricocheted from stone steps. The truck lurched up, stopped, and three men tumbled out. Dan had his revolver—no fake this time—out and blazing. He fired two shots. One man was winged, but he knew he had no chance. Through, by God, on account of that lousy Squire! The truck was one of the circulation trucks from Squire's newspaper, with picked gorillas. They'd been set on his trail downtown, had missed him and followed. A good hunch, catching him coming out of Harding's. Slugs tore his hat, and ripped through his coat.

But suddenly automobile brakes whined behind him. Shots of larger caliber thudded and rapped. Dan fired again, ducking in the shadows of a short alley. The newspaper delivery men whirled to face the new onslaught.

Dan thanked God for the unofficial escort that had contacted with him—not Ollendorff's cops, but undercover boys who, nowadays, were watching all the inside men. One of his attackers crashed face down and lay still. Dan held his fire. The other two ran. Dan scudded to the head of the alley. He shouted to the car by the curb:

"Hey!"

Four men piled out, dropping sawed-offs in the tonneau. The deserted truck stood in the street ten feet away. Dan recognized his rescuers; they had hovered around many places where he had been. Harding must have told them to shadow him when he left the Mayor's house so quickly.

In the distance, a police whistle shrilled. Lights came on in windows. The whole thing, lost among warehouses, had taken less than a minute.

Dan and two of the gunmen picked up the fallen newspaper truckman. They hove him into the truck, and the two gunmen drove off clangorously. "To the river!" one of them grunted.

Dan picked up his hat, and rearranged his coat. The other two gunmen drove him to Sixth Avenue, where he got out. There would be no trouble over this. "Thanks a lot, boys. That was close."

Their hard, waxen faces stared at him. They speeded off. He taxied to his hotel, safe and content.

In the morning, over a late breakfast, he read the *Press* from Page One to Page Forty-eight. There was nothing in it about a hold-up of the editor, or about a murder.

CHAPTER IX

By Hook or by Crook

DAN's natural interest, on Election Day, took him during the morning to Democratic Headquarters in a new office building on mid-town Broadway. But right after breakfast he had cast his vote in a booth in a barber shop on West Forty-eighth Street. From there he walked downtown, shoving his way through queues of people in front of other polling places. Apart from this slight obstruction to traffic, there was little to indicate that the population of New York City was dedicating the day to the election of a Mayor and all other municipal officials.

In Democratic Headquarters—a large office space given over to disordered heaps of pamphlets, brand new desks and a lot of persons who wandered about detachedly—there was noise and a feeling of confidence. But there was nobody Dan wanted to see.

He went over to the District Club, where he found Doyle, asleep in a chair, looking haggard. A few other tired men came and went and paid no attention. Dan kicked Doyle's protruding foot. The man stirred and grunted.

"Allez!"

"Go 'way, you goddam—"

"Come on! Tell me something!"

Doyle sat up painfully. He had evidently been hard at it the last two weeks. Purplish pouches hung under his doleful eyes, and his skin was gray. He stared at Dan, then said with sudden ferocity:

"Why in hell can't you lea' me alone?" Then he lit a cigarette and glared at the floor.

"Nuts! I want to know where the mob is."

"How do I know? I'm goddam near a dead man gettin' 'em elected. The hell with 'em!"

"Go home to bed, you frowsy politician," Dan told him genially.

Doyle melted. "Billy was supposed to go to Police Headquarters this morning. After that—" He shrugged.

Dan left him and went down to the office. He called Police Headquarters. "Where's the Commissioner?"

"He's here."

"Mayor Harding with him?"

"No!" Bang.

Somehow, Dan had neglected to ask where his friends would be, and now he felt absurdly lost. He wanted to cruise the city with Billy Harding and he couldn't find him. Oh, well, somebody would show up. He sat down and read a morning paper, the front page smeared with confident predictions of victory by everybody. He threw it away and looked out into the street. There was going to be only one victory, and that was Harding's. Maybe his last, Dan thought. He went to the phone and called the Mayor's home. He got Albert Firenze.

"This is Dan Fitzhugh. Where's Billy?"

"Here."

"Who else, Cheerful?"

"The Mrs." Pause. "Wait a minute." Mumble, mumble. "Billy says come for lunch. Lotta guys coming."

"Charming. I can't wait to see you." Bang.

Dan stalled around the rest of the morning and went to the Chelsea Park home at one o'clock.

The library was full of men, including most of the prominent candidates. Tully stayed for ten minutes after Dan arrived; Calloway and Dietrich went out together; and then most of them filtered out until only Firenze, Dan, Mrs. Harding and her spaniel and the Mayor were left. The room was gray with smoke, and Billy opened a window. Nobody had much to say. Harding was nervous. Firenze smoked and watched everybody, and Dan regretted he hadn't gone to see Lila, if only to hear her squawk. Which reminded him that he ought to go and put her mind at rest, now that the list was back again.

Mrs. Harding said into the silence: "If you win, Billy, I want to make another trip to Europe."

He was standing, his back to the room, staring into the street. "Sure."

"I hope you win."

"Thanks."

Silence again, until Harding turned to Dan. "Been to Headquarters?"

Dan nodded. "Everybody thinks it's in the bag."

Harding lit a cigar. "All this damn' talk. . . ."

Bella Harding said complacently: "I should think you would be more careful."

The Mayor's face turned ugly for a split second. Dan saw he hated her. Maybe because she had the fun and the money he wanted, without any of the headaches. Dan was sorry for him, briefly. To break the tension himself, Harding forced a smile and said to Dan:

"If we win this time, everything will be swell. We'll have to start shoving you up the ladder, Danny. Smart lad." He smiled with a proprietary air.

Dan clipped: "Wouldn't mind!" But he found his dislike of the Mayor's vacillating good nature surging up in him again. Luncheon was served.

The meal went quickly, because they all ate like nervous wolves. Harding's hand shook frequently under the suspense. Scarcely a word was said, and they could have been four individuals marooned there and hating each other. That was nearly true. Dan speculated on Mr. Plessing, mooning in a hotel suite all day—he didn't associate the German with any fixed occupation. Then his mind drifted to Helen, who was rehearsing.

The luncheon over, they separated to wash for the

arduous day ahead for the Mayor. At a signal from him, Dan followed him into his living suite, leaving the Italian with Bella. Once inside, Harding, his face working, said:

"Dan, for Christ's sake do me a favor. Keep that woman away from me. Talk to her or something, but don't let her make any more cracks like that. I'll sock her."

"Some other day, perhaps."

Harding, his face sullen, left him, throwing back over his shoulder: "Wait till I clean up, and then we'll go to Headquarters before we vote."

Dan waited. Half an hour later, they left the house together, with the Mayor's Scotch terrier. Behind them in the parlor were the Mayor's wife and the Mayor's secretary in a lifeless silence. Outdoors, Harding took a deep breath.

They drove in the Mayor's car up to Headquarters, which still presented the same aspect of impermanency, energy and helplessness. Harding smiled, joked, with everybody. The campaign workers brightened their worn faces, and some even gave out feeble little cheers. Billy and Dan left, after learning that telephone reports showed the voters flocking to the polls in all the solidly Democratic districts. This was a sure presage of victory.

They arrived back in Chelsea Park about three o'clock, and the first excitement was caused by the

Scotty fighting a short but noisy battle with Bella's spaniel. Harding kicked the spaniel across the room. Mrs. Harding called him something Dan couldn't catch, then picked up the whining dog and stroked it. Within fifteen minutes the doorbell rang. Out the window, Dan saw a police escort, all on foot, because the Mayor and his wife were going to vote at a Public School two blocks away. They should have voted first thing in the morning, that being the accepted tradition for men in high office, Dan reflected. But Billy Harding was notorious for being tardy at all public appearances.

The group left the house. A Police Captain saluted, and the procession started. A crowd collected at once, and a steady stream of commendatory comment surged around them.

"Our Billy! Go to it, kiddo, we're all for ya!"

Somebody shied a carrot. A policeman waved his nightstick. The approving cries redoubled until they reached the poll. A cordon of cops was thrown around the side doorway of the school. Photographers scurried up like crabs. The Mayor and Mrs. Harding posed for pictures, and then entered the building. In three minutes they had voted. They posed again, smiling, on either side of the booth containing the voting machine. A cheer burst forth as the flashlights smoked.

By a quarter to four they were back at home and Mrs. Harding, protesting a headache, went upstairs to

KVCC

KALAMAZOO VALLEY
COMMUNITY COLLEGE
LIBRARY

lie down. She had all she wanted for now of her husband. Firenze said:

"This is going to be a long evening. You better take a nap yourself, Billy."

Harding made no reply, but picked up the phone and called a number. Some one answered, and he said:

"Will you let me speak to Miss Faire, please. Helen Faire, yes. Very important. It's Mr. Firenze calling."

The Italian looked at him sideways.

"Hello, baby? Billy. How are you? Listen, kid, get this straight. What train do you take now? . . . One o'clock? Fine. I'll get news of the election to you by hook or by crook tonight, before you go. I know you're anxious, baby. Yeah, go on that train. I'm taking one at six—I have to be here all night, I told you—and I'll meet you at the theater in Boston by noon. We'll have lunch, or—what? No, no, it's all right. Now go back and rehearse. G'by."

Obviously, the Italian secretary hadn't known of this. The show was opening in Boston. Firenze said:

"I don't think that's such a smart trick."

Harding grinned: "Jesus, I have to have some fun. I'm tired, and to hell with this town for a few days! Who'll know? You just say I snuck away for a rest. That's your end."

They killed the afternoon, and a few minutes after six when the polls closed, the telephones started ringing. Headquarters and the different clubs were calling,

leaders from every city district, Tully, Ollendorff, Quinn, a dozen others repeatedly, all reporting an early and overwhelming lead for the reëlection of Mayor William T. Harding. The tension in the room gradually relaxed. It came seven o'clock, with the telephones still going, Harding lying down on a divan, smoking cigars, and Firenze doing the talking. Dan began to itch for action. None of them had noticed it was dinner time when Bella walked into the room.

"Billy, I'm hungry."

He jumped up, smiling. He was even nice to her. "I'm sorry, darling. Where do you want to eat? Bozo's out."

"I'm going to the hotel to change. You come for me there."

She left. Harding got into dress clothes, and Dan tried to stifle the boredom that kept creeping over him. Soon they left the house in the chill November darkness, and the panic was on. With two motorcycle policemen sirening their way through traffic, the big sedan whizzed to Mrs. Harding's hotel. She came down, and at the same time another car started following them, full of plainclothes men. They went to another hotel and all piled out. Mr. and Mrs. Harding were recognized in the dining room, and photographers caught up with them. More posing and smiling side by side. Then they ate, interrupted constantly by friends and strangers rushing up to congratulate genial Billy on his imminent victory. Mrs. Harding ate steadily, smiling mechanically. Luckily, they had no time to talk to each other.

In the big sedan again to the Municipal Building, way downtown. A radio address to the public by the almost reëlected Mayor of New York. That took an hour. Then they dropped Bella at her hotel in silence. Then to the Hall, where they caught the tail end of an informal dinner to Honest Tom Tully. Harding, grinning like a kid, walked up and shook hands with the leader, who smiled with thin-lipped satisfaction. A chair was brought for the Mayor, but before he could sit down, there came cries of, "Speech! Speech!"

He got up: "Fellow members, this is a great occasion and it warms my heart to see you all here, paying an honest, sincere tribute to the man who has made our victory today possible—Thomas Tully!"

Ringing cheers, banging of dishes and silver. Dan and Firenze found chairs further down the line. A peculiar attentiveness came in everybody's attitude—flushed faces sobered—when a stir at the door resolved into the entrance of Jim White, the Big Fellow. They recognized him at once, and a cheer started, feeble at first, then loud and lusty. Tully's face wore a casual smile, slightly patronizing in quality. Bowing, beaming, his jovial mouth under a rounded hook-beak split in a wide smile, Jim White walked to the head of the table.

Dan liked Jim White, as they all did, even if he was out of the political running. His medium-sized figure was strong, his eyes a twinkling blue, his skin mottled by frequent glimpses of crimson vintage. But that was Jim White's only vice. He was one of the shrewdest politicians in history; he had come from the waterfront to be Governor of New York State, and now he was in big business. He was tough, warm-hearted, religious and honest. Jim White shook hands cordially, first with Tom Tully, then with Harding. Both were eager, but the least bit offhand. Again cries of, "Speech!"

Jim White grinned. He seemed happy, because he had, after all, given his approval to the renomination of William T. Harding.

"Members o' the Hall—my friends—I wanna tell ya that this day is one of the bright ones o' my life. It does my heart good to see you boys put it over. I think ya got a great Mayor and a great leader. What more do ya want!"

Resounding cheers. Photographers. The biting smell of flashlight powder. A photographer burned himself. Harding stood up, looking at his watch. Just then an excited man came in the door. Everybody listened:

"We're in. We're in! Mayor Harding, Quinn, everybody! We can't lose now!"

An excited babble. This was premature, Dan knew. The returns couldn't all be in, but it was undoubtedly true. Harding grabbed his and Firenze's arms. Out they rushed. They had all had some drinks.

In the sedan, over to Democratic Headquarters. Delirious cheers from the same, worn, excited staff. Telephones rang, jangled, buzzed. Men shouted: "We can't lose, Billy!"

Harding cried, "Whoopee!" The fever was on them all. Dan felt his face beginning to ache from a steady grin. They went downstairs after liberal straight shots of Scotch from a bottle. In the street they found a mounted policeman. Harding rushed up to him.

"Listen, Officer, what's your name?"

The man looked down haughtily at being thus addressed, then frightened respect dawned on his face. "O'Flaherty, Mr. Harding, sir!"

"Listen, O'Flaherty, here's a job for you. Go over to the New Theater, stage door. Ask for Miss Helen Faire, tell her that Mayor Harding has been reëlected!"

"Yes, sir. Yes, Mr. Harding!"

"Here's a hundred dollars, Officer O'Flaherty. Now, hurry!"

Harding exploded with laughter when the sedan was again under way. "Wait till I tell Ollendorff this." He roared. "I promised her by hook or by crook!" He roared again. "You can't call that by hook, can you?" Firenze smiled, Dan grinned.

There were parties to go to. One at Julius Moses', the lawyer; another at a newspaper publisher's in a high tower-like building; another at the home of Nathan Steinmetz, great Jewish lawyer and close friend of Harding; another at a theatrical star's home. Everywhere, everybody was drunk or getting that way. Dan noticed nothing out of the way until about four-thirty A.M., when in getting out of the sedan—the motorcycle policemen had been sent away long ago—Harding almost fell on his face.

He and Firenze took him home. They packed a bag for him, as he lay on the divan, watching them with a glazed, vacant smile and saying now and again: "Mayor Harding in for his second term. I'll be a son of a bitch!" Then, "By hook or by crook!" And he roared.

They had a bag packed by five-fifteen. Down to the sedan again, and off to Grand Central Station. The Mayor sang, the Mayor whooped and was joyous. They only hoped he wouldn't be sick. They bought him a ticket, and stowed him away, in the care of a liberally tipped porter, in his compartment. He threw after them: "Good-by you lice. See you in—" he lurched against the bunk—"in hell!"

They left him, feeling woolly and hungry. They separated in the rotunda.

About one-thirty the next afternoon Dan read the papers.

Headlines screamed the Harding victory, the whole ticket having been swept into office by well-nigh overwhelming leads. Democratic candidates won everywhere. Judge Edward Quinn became District Attorney for New York County. Dan had a job for the next four years.

He read the story of how Tom Tully had received floods of telegrams and phone calls congratulating him on the Organization victory. Detailed stories told of their mad dashing around New York, up until the parties began. From then on, nothing. The Mayor's City Hall office announced that he had gone away for a rest after the ardors of the campaign.

An editorial said:

"The people of this great city have demonstrated their faith and confidence in Mayor William Tolliver Harding in an unmistakable way. He has had returned to him the mandate of the millions—to govern wisely and justly, in the eyes of the city, of the state, of the country and of the world. A gigantic task faces him: one, we are sure, of which he is keenly and sensitively aware. After a few days' rest, he will take up again where he has left off in his efforts to leave behind him a sterling record. Our best wishes!"

Dan was so used to that sort of thing, he didn't even laugh.

Six days later, at the beginning of the following week, the Mayor of New York returned to his own city, without fanfare or publicity. He had left the show in Boston, and for want of companionship that night, dropped into Lila's. Dan had come in for a Scotch and soda after a movie. The place was quiet, with only a few people sitting in the bar room. Lila took him and Dan into her own apartment. The secretary was off having his weekly Italian dinner with his own huge family downtown: Antipasto, minestrone, spaghetti, and hard-boiled eggs cooked in some strange bread.

Lila wanted to talk to Dan—he knew what about— but he stayed out of her way.

Harding relapsed in a chair and sighed.

"Good time, Billy?" Lila asked.

He perked up. "Say, let me tell you that's a great show! What girls! God, I never saw such shapes. That guy Tobin knows his onions."

Dan chuckled. "What the devil did you do, spend all your time in rehearsals?"

Harding swallowed some of his drink and made an elaborate shrug. "Certainly. I had a hell of a lot of fun. Forgot this damn' town and all its headaches. I relaxed. Boy, you wait'll that opera opens on Broadway!"

Lila sank back against the cushions on the chaise longue. "You're a hot sketch. Rehearsing a musical comedy. . . . How's Helen?"

Harding laughed boyishly. "Great. She's a clever kid, all right. Funny thing happened. She kept being late for rehearsals, and Tobin squawked at her. She tells him she has no watch. Then later some dame in the show says to her: 'Why don't you get Billy to give you a watch?' So she comes to me and says she wants a watch."

"Of course, you came through," Dan suggested.

"I didn't want to go in a jewelry store there. Might be recognized. So I'm sending her one tomorrow. One of the hundred and one watches different people gave me. You know, presentation watches. I picked out one I got from the Red Cross." He laughed. "Now she'll be on time." He finished his drink.

Dan grew interested in another angle. "How in hell did you keep under cover? My God, suppose the papers there had found out about you?"

Harding repeated his elaborate shrug. "I got pals, boy. I told 'em to leave me alone, and they left me alone. I like Boston newspaper men. And lemme tell you—it was great to feel I could walk around and not have people holler at me in the streets."

"You love it and you know it," Lila murmured.

"I enjoyed myself," he grinned shamelessly.

"You took a chance," Dan said.

Harding waved a hand with confident deprecation. "Forget it. We're in the bag."

CHAPTER X

Thrown to the Wolves

EVEN though nobody could put his finger on who had told De Angelis about Pasquale, the accusation was so definite it couldn't be overlooked. The Bar Association took it up and began its own inquiry. Of course that wasn't official, but it carried plenty of weight. The new Harding administration was sworn in on the first of January, and at the same time the City's most dignified legal body started to call witnesses before its investigating committee. There was no secret made of whether or not Pasquale actually had borrowed money from the dead gambler Rosenberg; he had admitted that without hesitation months before. The problem was to establish whether such traffic with the underworld constituted just grounds for the removal of a magistrate.

It began to look damning, at least from the findings of the unofficial but important Bar Association inquiry. So much so that the master minds thought best to announce a probe. Judge Quinn, almost as his first official move, stated that the District Attorney's office would coöperate with all agencies to discover the truth— which meant nothing. Right after that, the real trouble got under way in the Legislature, when State Senator Herman De Groodt demanded a formal investigation by the Appellate Division. And on the first of February the Bar Association heard its last witnesses; on the 16th it called for the immediate removal of Magistrate Antonio Pasquale. The grounds that he had borrowed money from Al Rosenberg, whether directly or indirectly, were held to be sufficient cause.

When this broke, the papers descended on Pasquale en masse and demanded a statement. He said:

"I do not believe that I have committed a crime, or even that I am guilty of malfeasance in connection with my office or my private life. I have no intention of resigning."

Tully got the boys together that very night. These sessions were getting to be frequent. Dan knew Honest Tom had called Quinn in on this, and he also knew that Quinn hadn't been informed that Tully had called Dan on the side. The boss told Dan over the phone:

"This is confidential. You show up with Judge Quinn, even though it's not customary. There may be things you can explain to him that we wouldn't have time to."

Dan recognized an extension of the reason which had assured himself, Blavitz and Ritchie of reappointments to their jobs. Quinn was not too smart.

On his arrival at Tully's home, Dan was surprised to find one of the less familiar figures there: State Supreme Court Justice Eugene Kendall. The latter was a medium-sized, undistinguished-looking man, bald half-

way back on his head, with pale grayish eyes and a
weak mouth. Kendall, Dan knew, came in when the
higher courts were involved. He was also important
because he sat on city land condemnation proceedings,
which always were necessary when the municipality was
buying sites for bridges, schools, new subway stations
and what not. It was part of the game to see that the
boys owned plots in strategic places.

Kendall nodded to Dan. Tully, Harding, Quinn,
Firenze and Pasquale made up the rest of the group.

Pasquale, whom Dan knew but very slightly, reminded him of De Angelis. Short, heavily built, intense
black eyes with deep olive-green spots on them, Pasquale couldn't hide his Italian origin. He used a low
voice, and his stubby hands massaged each other.

They sat around, and Tully went right into it:

"We've got something serious on our necks. Not exactly ruinous, but it's got to be handled quickly. Now,
I'm going to ask a question—" he directed himself to
the magistrate— "and I want a snappy answer."

The Italian, sitting in a low easy leather chair beside a table, fidgeted. "I guess I'm in a tough jam,"
and he tried to smile, looking around at the faces of his
friends and allies.

"Here's the question," Tully's thin lips framed.
"Why did you give out that statement this morning?"

The magistrate blinked and made a vague gesture
with his paws. "I—I had to say something."

Harding: "That wasn't the crack to make. You

should have said——" He fell silent when Tully raised a hand.

The chief growled: "The point right now isn't whether or not you're guilty, but what you mean by going ahead on your own hook this way. How do you expect us to do anything when you're talking wildly all over the place?"

Pasquale babbled: "My God, what do you expect me to do? I am caught unawares. I am left to myself. Out of a blue sky comes this accusation. Where did that man, De Angelis, find out? Still, there is no proof."

"Then why did you admit it?" Quinn, the lawyer, put in a finger. "If there wasn't any proof, why didn't you wait?"

"I thought I did the best thing."

"You're a fool," Tully spat at him. The magistrate's eyes began to widen with fear. "Now, I'm telling you you had no business talking so much without consulting us. Who put you in that job?"

Silence was heavy on them all, but Dan sensed drama ahead.

Tully's cool, angry voice went mercilessly on: "It will be very difficult for us to save you. There is only one way for you not to be badly disgraced. But I am not thinking of you."

Harding, looking a little scared, watched Tully. Dan wondered what the Mayor was thinking. Firenze had his eyes on his countryman, and Kendall sat unobtrusively. Dan asked himself where the Supreme Court Justice came into it.

Kendall suddenly answered Dan's mental question. "See here, Tom, there's only one thing to do." Everybody looked at him. "I don't think you can stall off an Appellate Division inquiry on this."

Tully peered at him. Pasquale almost pleaded with his eyes. Kendall continued: "I don't see how you can do it. The charge was specific and admitted. Even if it can't be proved, that admission can't be denied now. It's received too much unfavorable publicity."

Pasquale stood up nervously: "I don't think you guys wanta get me outa this!" He glared.

"Sit down!" Tully's blood was up. "We can't save you now. You're finished. I'm thinking of the Hall. You've got your money, and you can go to Europe, or stay right here. Who cares? But we're in line to be blamed for your foolishness. Now—"

Pasquale sneered: "I thought this outfit existed just to straighten out such things!"

"Oh, did you?" Tully's cold eyes glittered. "Now you're finding out differently."

Quinn, his old gray eyes inquisitive, leaned over and touched Dan's arm. Dan stooped near him, and the D.A. whispered: "They could save him, I think. I'd like to tell them how."

Dan shook his head. "Maybe. But don't. He's going overboard."

Quinn, looking disappointed, sat back and said very little more the rest of the evening. Harding put in an oar:

"Tom, as I see it, the only way to stop the whole business is to have him resign, right off. That would show a willingness to stand trial."

Everybody, except the two Italians, nodded. Pasquale walked across the room and faced them.

"A fine goddam lot of friends! What the hell am I going to do, take the rap for all of you? I'm not the only one on that list, and don't forget it!"

"Shut up!" from the Mayor.

Tully cracked: "You keep your mouth shut, Pasquale! You talk too much. The more you talk, the less we help you."

The stocky magistrate's thick lips twisted. "Help me! You make me laugh!"

The leader pointed a forefinger at him. "Here's what's going to happen. When we get through here, you see the papers. Tell them you have reconsidered your decision of last night, and will resign, ready to stand trial and be vindicated."

"The hell I'll do that!" he flamed.

"The hell you won't!" Harding looked helplessly at Tully who got up and went out of the room. In a moment he returned with a sheaf of papers in his hand. Dan's heart jumped. Here was the Rosenberg list again, and those he had lifted it for had, after all, turned it over to the chief. Tully sat down in his chair again and looked at the papers.

"I've got this figured out. We're going to send the Rosenberg list back to Brand."

Harding was on his feet. "Hey, for Christ's sake!" His face showed panic in his heart. Kendall's hands and feet moved nervously.

Tully smiled. "Sit down. Do you think I'm crazy? This isn't the real list." They breathed again, but not quite easily yet. "I've had a new one fixed up. The original has enough political names on it to blow us all up—" his eyes roved to Harding, Kendall and Pasquale— "but this one has only one, besides a lot of people we don't care about." The atmosphere tightened suddenly again.

Tully leaned forward and said softly: "Mr. Pasquale is through. We all understand that. Very well, we will clinch the matter. This list has, of the important ones, only Pasquale's left on it." Tully looked round at everybody. Pasquale stared like a cobra about to attack. "We will arrange to have this list mysteriously sent back to Brand. Maybe he will, privately, show it to someone. In any event, it is not his having the list which will remove Pasquale; but the knowledge that the list contains his name will have a powerful effect on everyone. You follow me?"

After a few seconds' pause he went on: "Brand can't use the list, then, politically, as we suspect he wants to for his coming gubernatorial campaign. Also, it will settle the matter of the list once and for all, and stop people thinking about it."

Dan glanced round. Quinn seemed horrified. Harding had no expression. Kendall seemed to want to say something, but didn't. Pasquale broke the tension.

"You goddam double-crossers! You'd pull a lousy trick like that on me! By Jesus Christ, I'll tell everybody who was on the list! I'll spill the whole story! You stinkin'—" He suddenly had a small bronze statuette in his hand, lifted off a bookcase. His eyes showed the whites.

Firenze, in two steps, was across the room. His fist flicked and a crack told he had hit the button. Pasquale staggered, and his lips were bleeding. The secretary wrenched the statuette from his hand and replaced it, keeping his narrowed eyes on the magistrate. Unexpectedly Pasquale sobbed, rage tearing in his throat. Then he sat down, his eyes on the floor, a handkerchief wiping away the blood.

Tully went on: "That's useless. Now, Firenze, you send a man with this list to Brand's office. You know, some nondescript person, just to drop it there, without their knowing how it got back. You understand?"

Albert nodded. "Sure." He crossed and took the list from Tully and put it in his pocket.

"Now, we're clear, are we?" Tully looked round. He was the only one, except Dan, who was calm. "You—"

he addressed the cowed magistrate—"tell the papers tonight that you are resigning. File your resignation with the Chief Magistrate in the morning. Then wait for trial and take what's coming to you. I earnestly advise you not to do anything else rash." He stared, and Pasquale understood him.

Dan asked: "What about the original of the list?"

Harding laughed: "Forget it, Dan."

"Why? I lifted it, and I want to know."

Tully answered him: "We have it safely. There may come a use for it some other time."

Dan sat back. He was thinking of his own copy in the hotel safe. The thing was little good to him now. Anyway, he didn't want to give it to Portis, who would get too excited. He looked at Firenze, who was giving all his attention to the magistrate. Dan decided he had better get rid of his list and forget it, as Harding advised.

Tully said: "So far as I'm concerned, we're finished for this evening. Is there anything on anybody's mind?"

Kendall brought up a new topic: "Who gets Pasquale's place?"

"Oh, that's hard to say. There are a lot of good men in the Bronx. Brunner, for example."

The Supreme Court Justice shrugged. "Then, one more thing, when're you going ahead with the Seventy-fifth Street Hudson Bridge?"

Harding answered: "We'll have plans soon, then

estimates. I should think we could spring the thing in March some time."

Somebody said: "Well, let us know."

Somebody else laughed. Pasquale got up and faced them: "I'm going now. I'll do as you tell me. But listen to this. You're a bunch of crooked, stinking gyps." He walked out, and left them thinking it over.

Tully sighed audibly: "Well—"

They broke up. Everybody was relieved. A man had gone overboard to save the rest and he wasn't getting any compensation for taking the rap, because he'd talked too much. Dan walked home, a couple of miles, but he felt energetic.

He got some satisfaction out of finding that he had been right in thinking that pinning something on Pasquale would start something. He had known it would, and he wondered considerably how Tully could think that throwing one man to the wolves for them to worry to death would stop the trouble. Dan had a feeling that plenty more people were going to get in trouble after this—Heaven alone knew who, because sooner or later the thing was going to get beyond anybody's control. Sooner or later, too, it would get to the Mayor. And that's what Portis wanted.

Dan gave deep thought to his copy of the Rosenberg list. The dick who had lifted it from the gambler's safe had been shot in a gang battle soon after Ollendorff's man had found out about him. Dan could give the list to Portis as ammunition, but he concluded it was too soon. The Mayor of New York was in too impregnable a position now to be so easily reached. Magistrates were easy. They were close to the public, but the Mayor was on a pedestal. When the pedestal was proven rotten—the throne would begin to totter.

Viewed in that light, the list was no good and too dangerous. He went to his hotel to get it out of the safe. They handed him the envelope and he went upstairs.

He opened the envelope and took out a sheaf of perfectly blank sheets of paper. That was all. He sweated.

He couldn't squawk to the hotel, because he couldn't tell them what had been in the envelope. He admired the ingenuity of putting in blank paper, because whoever had done it had figured just that way. It must have been done through one of the clerks, but it didn't make much difference which one. He couldn't do anything. No point.

He lay awake most of the night, feeling that his future was precarious. Who the devil knew he had made a copy? He had cold perspiration on his forehead and, to make himself feel better he put his revolver under his pillow. Then he cursed out loud at himself for a fool and put it back in his valise under the bed. They'd get him if they wanted him.

He thought perhaps Firenze had done it.

CHAPTER XI

A Typical Harding Day

DAN began to wonder whether being on the inside, as much as he was getting to be, was worth it. He got let in for all sorts of things. And Mayor Harding's publicity tour wasn't the least of them. It started innocently enough, with the Mayor telephoning him from City Hall the morning of April 15th. Dan had been wondering how to get off to attend the opening of the baseball season—Giants and Braves—at the Polo Grounds. Harding said to him over the phone:

"Can you knock off work, Dan?"

"What's up?"

"Tell Quinn I need you with me today. I got a lotta places to go, and I need company."

"How about little Albert?"

Pause. "He's busy some place. Come on with me. I have to go to the ball game. Meet me for lunch at the Town Club, on Forty-fourth Street."

"Okay."

It developed at the Town Club that a testimonial luncheon was being given to a transatlantic flyer. He and Harding were placed at the speakers' table. Harding was called on for a speech. He stood up, talking into the microphone:

". . . And let me tell you, ladies and gentlemen, not the least of the pleasures of being Mayor of the people of the City of New York is meeting the great and famous persons who come here. No other town on the face of this wonderful earth can welcome as we do in New York, and it becomes my humble duty to extend to our honored guest here today the cordial felicitations of the millions of our great community."

The cameras clicked, and he sat down.

They chatted amiably with men who fawned and smiled and joked badly. Dan was just getting bored when Harding looked at his watch.

"Come on, boy. We're off!" They shook hands with dozens of men and women. Applause rattled in their ears as they walked out through the crowded tables. Then they were in the Mayor's sedan, rolling smoothly uptown toward the Polo Grounds.

"Say," demanded Harding when they reached One Hundred and Twenty-fifth Street, "who was that fellow, anyway?"

"Who, the aviator?"

"Was he an aviator?"

They both laughed. The car deposited them at the entrance of the Polo Grounds. They went into the club house and spoke to the players. Harding knew them all. He introduced Dan to the heavy, gray-haired manager of the Giants. At a signal, the Mayor of New York led the parade of baseball players with their brass band, and a number of minor city officials, from the club house to the diamond. There they played the *Star Spangled Banner*, and escorted the Mayor to his box. He leaned over and threw the first ball of the New York baseball season. Fifty thousand people cheered. The Mayor waved his gray felt hat, and photographers scurried. They watched six innings of a corking ball game. The Giants were leading four to two at the beginning of the seventh when Harding took a glance at his watch.

"Let's get a move on, Dan. Board of Estimate meeting at five. How those birds hate for me to set one as late as that. Ha, ha! We have twenty minutes." They left the Polo Grounds, Dan wanting to stay.

"Go on to your meeting. I want to see the rest of this game."

Harding laughed indulgently and seized his arm to hurry him along. "No, you don't. We've got a dinner to go to, and after that, a swell party. Helen's giving it in her new place. Housewarming."

"All right."

In thirty-five minutes of breakneck driving the car landed them at the Board of Estimate meeting in the City Hall. Dan went home to his hotel to dress for dinner while Harding went into the meeting, smiling, bowing, especially nice to more photographers.

In three quarters of an hour Dan was waiting in the car when the Mayor emerged. They went to his Chelsea Park home for Billy to climb into a tuxedo. While dressing, he talked:

"God, boy, we put one through today!"

"Didn't think there was time for anything. You mean the Seventy-fifth Street Bridge plan went through?"

"Well, not through, exactly, but the first appropriation is in the bag. Twenty million dollars." He tied his black tie and brushed his trousers. "Hey, do me a favor and tell Helen on the phone we'll be there around eleven."

Dan telephoned. Helen was out. He left a message and returned to the bedroom to find the Mayor ready. He wore a frown on his habitually grinning face. They went downstairs and Dan was surprised to hear him order the driver to take them to Tom Tully's.

Dan said: "I didn't know we were going there."

Harding hesitated before he said: "Well, this bridge appropriation has me worried. See, a lot of the boys have land around there, but I'm the guy who put the plan up. If anything goes wrong, it's all on me. I don't know as I like it."

"Oh, why worry? What's wrong if somebody's friends happen to own land where a bridge is going to be built? Somebody has to own it." He felt a ready sympathy—that perverse liking for Mayor Harding that, fundamentally, he most often felt. The Mayor said:

"Yeah, I know, but— Well, I'm goin' to talk to Tom about it anyway! You don't mind if we're a little late for that dinner?"

Dan declared he didn't mind. "What's the idea of all this rushing around so publicly?"

Harding looked at him sidewise. "You can't figure it out? You're not as dumb as that?"

Dan thought. Publicity touring, frequently resorted to if the front page wasn't given to the Mayor often enough, meant that publicity of the right, innocuous kind was needed. Why was it needed? That was easy. Because the flamboyant, faintly ridiculous antics of Police Commissioner Frank Ollendorff had been grabbing all the space.

Ollendorff, the Big Noise, the ex-bus-line executive, had made little secret of his desire for publicity. He personally attended to the installation of new traffic stations, attired in top hat and Chesterfield. He rushed to the scenes of big accidents and sensational crimes. He gave interviews at the drop of a hat, and hats dropped easily. He had a flair for inflating the slightest item of news into something big. He was at once impressive, spectacular and absurd. Which made him good copy. Harding had to combat it, because now the menace was growing sinister, as revealed in Harding's next words to Dan as they spun on their way to the boss of the Hall:

"Fact is, Ollie thinks he can be Mayor of New York. Tie that."

"Oh, for God's sake!" Dan laughed. He felt in him a keen though obscure regret that Harding, the man doomed to disgrace, was such a pleasant fellow.

"Of course it's nothing but a joke, and a bum one. But it could make a lot of trouble in the organization. Ollie believes it himself."

"Then he'll have to be tossed over. He's a lousy Commissioner."

"Sure, he'll go. It won't be long."

"You know the Department is getting rotten under him? I don't think he even knows it."

Harding grimaced. "The next one'll be a cop, in that case."

"A cop!" Dan stared at him amazedly. "The hell you say. Why?"

Harding looked out of the window. They were nearing Tully's. "Oh, a lot of reasons! It would look good, and won't attract so much attention."

"Sure, I know, but—" Then he saw Harding didn't want to talk any more. The Mayor moved, preparing to get out. They turned a corner and stopped.

They found Tully in the middle of dinner. They walked in. Dan was surprised, Harding disconcerted, to find Jim White a guest. In typical courtly fashion Harding apologized to Mrs. Tully for the intrusion.

"I've got a few words to say to you, Tom. Can we talk?"

Tully nodded. The three men went into the library. White stayed behind. Harding talked without looking at the boss. "Today we put through the bridge site appropriation."

Tully brightened. "The bridge will be a good thing on your record. Very good."

"Yes, but there's this angle to it. The boys own land all around there. Almost every one of them."

"Well, that's happened before."

Dan watched Tully. Harding continued, a bit nervously: "I know, I know! But what I don't like is this: it's all been done on my responsibility alone."

"Well, Good Lord, why not?"

Harding stood up. He raised his eyes to meet Tully's. "The hell with why not! If anything goes flooey, who takes it on the chin? I do, all alone."

"Well?"

"I don't like it a bit. Either we kill that damn' thing, or somebody else comes in on the responsibility with me. Understand?"

Dan felt a secret astonishment at Harding's determination. This was something new in the man which he hadn't expected. Tully kept silence while many seconds clicked off. Harding stared at him belligerently.

Tully finally said quietly: "I don't see what you've got to complain about, Billy. The bridge is a fine and progressive move in itself. If there's profits on the side for a few people who happen to own land there, that's got nothing to do with you."

"Oh, no!" Harding rapped at him. "Only I was the one who advocated moving it down to Seventy-fifth from Eighty-fifth and there's plenty of smart guys can figure out it was because up there the land is hard to get."

"So what do you want me to do?"

Dan was waiting for the blow. There was something wrong with this picture. Harding explained: "Appoint a board of engineers to examine new sites. Something like that. Jesus, this angle just struck me today, and with all this stink over magistrates breaking, who the hell knows what will happen?"

Tully's words came fast: "You make me tired. You don't see that if they ever get to you, you won't go down alone. You'll have all the company you want."

Harding made a scornful sound. Tully snapped:

"All right, if that's how you feel. Now, get this. You're in there as Mayor to do just those things. You let somebody else do the worrying. We've got trouble enough without listening to squawks from people like you."

Harding started to talk, but Tully cut him off. "I don't want to hear any more of that from you. You do as you're told, and I'll worry for you. Is that understood?"

"Aw, you've got me wrong, Tom!" Harding said appeasingly. "I didn't mean—"

"I know what you meant! Now I'm going back to my dinner. I hope you didn't spoil it for me. Good night, Dan."

In a very unpleasant and oppressive silence, Dan and the rebuffed and chastened soldier from the ranks marched out of the house.

The car moved slowly now through traffic toward the Astor Hotel.

"Well, what the hell?" Dan remarked after a long time.

Harding burst out venomously: "I'll be a son of a bitch if they'll make a goat out of me! Crandall, Jessup, Pasquale and some others, but not me, boy! Let 'em get that in their heads!"

"Somebody's got to do the dirty work. You're safe."

"Yeah, I'm safe all right! Maybe! But I don't want to be bossed around. It's okay for a dope like Quinn to say: 'My predecessor made such a mess of the Rosenberg case that I cannot do anything,' but—"

"That was good politics, don't forget."

"Sure it was. But excuses like that won't get *me* out of jams."

"There won't be any jams for you, Billy."

They arrived at the Astor Hotel, and went into the Grand Ballroom. A dinner for a prominent actor was

on. The Mayor and Dan sat at the speakers' table.
Harding said into the microphone:

". . . Most of us here tonight, and most of those
who are listening, have little enough of brightness, happiness and contentment in their lives. We have to fight
for everything we get. We have to overcome all the
obstacles in our paths. But there are in the world many
whose task it is to bring lightness and brightness to
others. I mean our honored guest here this evening. We
are not gathered here to tell him he is a pleasant fellow.
Nor to tell him that we like his face. We are here to
represent those thousands who have been the recipients
of his great gift: that of making his fellow humans
laugh. That, fellow citizens, is a sacred act."

There were more speeches, more laughs, photographers, until the dinner broke up about eleven-thirty.
Harding hustled Dan out with him, and from the
dinner they also brought others—extemporaneous
guests at Helen's housewarming. She welcomed them at
the door of her six-room apartment with screams:

"Hello, hello, hello! You're late, you bad boy! H'lo,
Dan! H'lo, ev'rybody! Come on in! Throw your stuff
in that closet. You know everybody. Every man for
himself!"

Already some twenty people were there, chiefly
Harding's younger political friends and theatrical people. Dan recognized several actors, actresses, movie
directors, authors and playwrights. Drinks flowed

quickly, and Dan and Billy drank fast, both to catch up with the rest and to forget the day they had had. Harding lurched up to Dan after they had been there about an hour.

"Say, boy, I clean forgot to thank you for tailin' after me all day. It was lousy."

"Not so bad, Billy." Dan smiled at the Mayor's blearing eyes. He marveled at a man who could drink so much and hold it so badly.

"Ah, it was lousy! C'n y'magine that bum tellin' me where ta get off? The son of a bi— And Jim! Jesus, I'm glad—"

"I wouldn't talk about it here, Billy," Dan cautioned.

"An'—hmph!" Harding went into another room. Helen passed Dan. Her eyes were wild, her hair disarranged. A new evening dress fitted her loosely, the shoulder straps kept sliding off, and she often forgot to put them back in time. More guests came in, others left. It grew later and later. And Dan kept an eye on the door, thinking Lila might come. He hadn't seen her for a long time and he didn't want to now. Firenze came, stayed only a short while and brought up the subject:

"Lila says she hasn't seen you for a while."

"No. I been trailing after Quinn. Explain for me, will you?"

"Sure." And the Italian left him, smiling and knowing, Dan felt, that he hadn't been told the truth.

Dan talked to a lot of girls. But it was hard to make headway with most of those who were there. They were handpicked by Helen and watched their step. Dan finally found a friend and fed her drinks hopefully until she crossed him by passing out. He sent her home with another girl. He was growing disgusted after this episode, when he noticed only a few people were left. Two girls, one of whom departed right away, Ritchie, Harding, Helen and himself. Dan went into the front room to find Helen and Harding in a fierce argument.

"You oughtn' ta talk tha' way." Harding teetered and regarded his girl friend owlishly.

Helen screamed at him from where she was standing by a modernistic brown-and-red-desk: "Ah, you, you can't order me around! You're not payin' fer this!"

Dan jerked his head at Ritchie, who took the hint and went out, taking the other girl with him. Harding was very drunk and so was Helen. The Mayor waved a finger at her. "You talk to me like that any more 'n' I'll break your dirty neck. Tha's what."

Her face contorted in reasonless, intoxicated rage. "You'll break my neck? Well, I'd like to see you!" Her shoulder strap slipped and Dan could see the outline of her breasts, moving in agitated breathing.

Harding started toward her, his face red from drink and anger. "You'll keep your mouth shut when I get—"

Dan jumped. "Hey!"

Helen had opened a drawer of her desk. Something

gleamed in her hand. A shot crashed in the smoke-laden air of the over-decorated room. Dan tore the revolver from her hand and sent her spinning against the desk. She cried out in pain.

He found Harding looking at him in amazement. The Mayor's right hand went slowly to his left shoulder and his face twisted in a spasm. Then he pitched forward on his face.

Dan picked him up without waiting for anything else to happen. He put him on the bed in Helen's room, ripped off the clothes, and found a small bullet hole in the shoulder, through the flesh only, and probably not serious. He put a cold-water-soaked towel on it and went to the telephone to call the Mayor's doctor.

"Little accident. Come over to Miss Faire's apartment." The physician promised immediate arrival.

Dan went back to the Mayor who was lying flat on the bed, eyes wide open, staring terrified at the ceiling. He looked at Dan helplessly.

"What happened?"

"Helen plugged you. Nothing much, I don't think. Doctor'll be here in a minute."

Dan recalled Helen. He found her, still drunk, hanging on to the door jamb, staring in fixedly. Stark fear was in her eyes, but when Dan spoke to her she seemed not to hear him. Her hands were cold when he touched them.

"Come on, fix yourself up. The doctor's coming."

She didn't do or say anything, but just stared like an idiot. Dan grabbed her and half-carried her into the bathroom, where he turned on the cold shower. Then he stripped her and dumped her into the tub. She struggled feebly, but he pushed her under the shower. He swore at her when she splashed him.

Suddenly she woke up. "What the hell, you—?" Her nails scratched at him.

He pulled her out, wrapped a robe around her and deposited her in the other of the twin beds. Harding still lay waiting on the bed. He merely watched when Dan put Helen on the other bed and threw a blanket over her. She shivered, and again fixed her scared gaze on her fallen boy friend.

Dan let the doctor in when he rang—a small, dapper man who never asked questions. Which was why he had been Harding's doctor for several years. Dan told him that a toy pistol had gone off by accident. The physician nodded, pronounced it a trivial wound, at which Harding grunted with relief, bandaged it up tightly, and told the Mayor he was fit in every way.

Harding spoke unexpectedly: "Jesus, Dan, I have to be at City Hall at nine! I got to." He was cold sober now.

"All right. It's only five-thirty."

Silence. Dan looked at the girl. The blanket outlined her figure. She had the blanket up to her chin and she stared without blinking. Dan went to the living room, cluttered with glasses, bottles, overflowing ash trays, dried sandwiches, all the litter of a party. He threw open the window and lay down on the divan. He slept soundly until eight o'clock, when he went in and woke up Harding.

He helped him to dress, in clothes of his own Dan found in a closet, despite Harding's steady whining protests of pain. "Damn that bitch! This is a hell of a thing! Ow, look out!" But finally Dan got him shaved, dressed and ready. Just as they were leaving the bedroom, Harding turned and went to Helen. She only watched, though not so scared now. Her hair lay flat on her head, and she had deep purple shadows under her eyes.

Harding ground out savagely: "Damn' near forgot you! You dumb animal! I'd like to—" He raised a fist. Dan started to move. But Helen brought a bare arm out from under the cover. In a small, pitiful voice she said:

"Aw, Billy, I—I'm sorry." The blanket slipped a little bit, revealingly. Her hand stroked Harding's face, tickled his ear. "Kiss me, Billy. Please—forgive me." She drew his head down. Harding kissed her, first reluctantly, then with a chuckle, his rage forgotten. One hand seized her bare shoulder.

Dan turned away.

Outside they had a cup of coffee in Childs, then entered a cab. Harding grabbed Dan's arm: "Hey, how in hell am I gonna explain this away?"

"I've been thinking. You tell 'em you slipped on the soap in the bath tub and hurt your shoulder."

The Mayor stared at him angrily. "Are you nuts?"

"Tell 'em that. Take it from me."

"Nobody'll believe that."

Dan grew exasperated. "All right! Tell 'em Helen plugged you in a drunken brawl. But the other yarn is good. Insurance companies'll tell you people break arms and legs that way every day."

The Mayor subsided. The cab took them down Park Avenue. The buildings reflected dazzlingly the morning sun. Private cars, bearing prosperous owners, rolled silently along. The Mayor, his eyes red, his lips sagging, stared out dully. Dan lit a cigarette and felt of his unshaven chin. They spoke no more till Dan helped the Mayor out of the cab and they entered Harding's office in City Hall. Firenze was there, talking in the anteroom to four other men from other departments. Harding walked past them with an attempt at his usual geniality. Dan said:

"Take care of him, boys. He slipped in the bath tub this morning and hurt his shoulder."

CHAPTER XII

Baited with a Stool Pigeon

THROUGH the medium of the sexless secretary, Dan got one of his frequent calls from Colonel Portis one afternoon in June. He couldn't get away till the next afternoon, which was Saturday, and accordingly he went up to the office about four o'clock. No one was there except Portis. On his desk the Colonel had copies of almost all the morning and afternoon papers, all carrying prominently featured the Mayor's announcement of the appointment of Deputy Chief Inspector Cornelius (Connie) Dolan to the Commissionership of Police. The financier laid a forefinger on the papers and said:

"This is a terrible thing, Mr. Fitzhugh. What can be done about it?"

"Just like that!" Dan thought. But he said aloud: "What's so bad about it?"

Indignation welled up in Portis. "Why—it is infamous! From what you have told me of the increasing corruption in the Police Department under Ollendorff, I don't see how such a man, from the ranks, can be appointed to the top. It's an outrage."

"Oh, wait a minute. Dolan is a pretty honest man.

Of course, he'll take his orders from City Hall, but you can bet he's neither as stupid nor as ignorant as Ollendorff. After all, Ollie wasn't crooked. He was just dumb. Besides, I guess I told you how he thought he could be Mayor. They squelched that quick enough."

"I should hope so, indeed! I fail to see what can be expected of a man like Dolan. Ollendorff was bad enough, Lord knows, but—"

Dan tried to calm him. "I suggest you suspend judgment on Connie Dolan. He's a good honest Irishman. Only I'm a little sorry for him. He'll have to stay in the background. He'll do it, too, and I'd not be surprised if, in his quiet way, he greatly increased the efficiency of the Police Department."

Portis paused a long time before he broached the next topic. He spoke slowly:

"I think I can appreciate your viewpoint. I am seeing much more now, about the politics of our city, than I did before we began our work together. Individuals are culpable, I am getting to understand, rather than conditions. Or, to put it another way, individuals create amenable conditions. Therefore, it is all a matter of honest or dishonest, competent or incompetent, persons being in the proper positions of authority. That brings me to something I have wanted to ask you—" He looked at Dan squarely. "I do not quite understand your motives in working for me. I accepted at the beginning what you told me as being adequate, but I had no notion of the magnitude or perilous nature of our task. You gave me—"

Dan cut in coldly: "I gave you three good reasons. Good from my point of view, that is, and that were on the dead level. One: Mayor Harding took away from me a girl I was very, very fond of. That's a sentimental reason. Two: I was promised by Mayor Harding a nomination to the State Legislature. When Boss Walters objected to me, Harding withdrew his support, but he never mentioned the matter to me again. That's revenge. Three: You are going to pay me one hundred thousand dollars. That's gain."

The financier, a more kindly look in his eyes than Dan had ever seen there before, drummed with his fingertips on the desk. "They don't sound—ah—strong enough. Can't you give me another?"

Dan shook his head. He hadn't any other reasons, and he couldn't see the need of any. He owed nothing to the men above him, and this he tried to make clear to Portis. For everything they had given him, which was little enough, they had received full measure on his regular job, as well as outside work.

"My reasons are strong enough for me," he said. "Let's forget it."

"Forgive me if I have—ah—"

"It's okay. Anything else we ought to talk about?"

"Yes. I am disappointed in the resignation of Magistrate Pasquale. I had hoped for much more."

"Much more what? I don't get you."

"We-ell, that there would be more serious consequences to the De Angelis accusation and the subsequent trial of the man before the Appellate Division. His resignation and official removal is hardly enough." Dan thought back to Tully's confidence that throwing the Italian judge to the wolves would satisfy them. Portis continued with deliberation. "The whole situation appears to be at a standstill. But I tell you, Mr. Fitzhugh, I won't let it remain so. Something else has got to be done."

"You don't have to do anything."

"What do you mean?"

"The fuse is fired, that's what I mean. You got Pasquale, and I told you then it would start a stink. Well, it did, didn't it? Now, charges will be made by lots of people against other magistrates. There's plenty of dirt on how George Brunner—he used to be an Assistant District Attorney—got his job to fill Pasquale's place on the bench. I shouldn't say dirt, exactly, but he can be nailed on a question of ethics. He got the appointment by contributing heavily to the political society that recommended him to Harding. It's honest but not ethical, if you follow me. They're getting curious about conditions in the Magistrates' courts now, and that'll get plenty of 'em in trouble. Trouble's already been started against two more of the Italian magistrates. Did you instigate that?"

Colonel Portis shook his head.

"There you are. If all this business looks too bad, Adams will have to do something, or the Legislature will. I was guessing at that when I told you what I did about Pasquale. There's Kendall, Supreme Court Justice. He's mixed up in bridge site condemnations that would be hard to explain to an inquiry jury. You take it from me, none of them would ever be in trouble if it hadn't been for the Pasquale business."

"I imagine you're right. But I'm not sure. We must find another means of pushing matters faster. Now, I have been up to Albany to speak to Governor Adams."

This was getting big.

"I asked him what might happen if conditions became so disgraceful that public indignation was at length aroused. He told me that his only course then, when the Legislature approves the action, is to appoint a Special Commissioner. He spoke very highly of Judge Cullen Martineau. He has already made up his mind to choose him, should immediate developments demand it. Do you know Judge Martineau?"

"Not personally, but he's got a wonderful reputation. He's a Democrat, but not in the Hall. He's a former Supreme Court Justice. Great man for the spot."

Colonel Portis nodded with satisfaction. "I am glad to hear you speak of him in that manner. I have found your judgments of men most accurate."

"Thanks."

"Yes, on the whole Governor Adams was very sympathetic to my ideas. He believes, unofficially, of course, that the time has come for a drastic step. Now, what can we do to bring things to a crisis?"

"That's hard to say. Does Adams expect to appoint Martineau right away, or is that just a vague hope?"

"He said that the appointment of Martineau, or someone like him, is almost inevitable by the Fall."

"Well, we've got time. If they want dirt on Magistrates' courts, I can't think of a better way to dig it up than by getting a stool pigeon to talk."

Portis' stern blue eyes were baffled. "What?"

Dan expounded easily. He had just had the idea, and it wasn't bad. "Get a stool pigeon to talk. It's this way. While Ollendorff was Commissioner, the Vice Squad, which pinches prostitutes and so forth, used these men to help them make arrests. In other words, since it's tough for plainclothes dicks, whose faces get to be known, to catch girls red-handed, they employ these guys to pick up girls, go home with them, and then be the 'unknown man' when the cops walk in. That clear?

"The Vice Squad has always used this method, but under Ollendorff it got out of hand. I doubt if Ollie knew anything about it, but it's a fact that many magistrates were in on the racket. Shyster lawyers, too, and professional bondsmen. It's been a sweet racket, and they've all been getting away with it. Now, we'll

get one of these birds to spill all he knows. Any stool
pigeon will talk for a thousand dollars and a guarantee
of immunity."

Portis squawked: "How can you suggest such a
thing, Mr. Fitzhugh? We cannot stoop to methods of
that sort! It is impossible. How would it be, if it became known that the People's Franchise Union had
bribed an underworld character to reveal his crimes?"

Dan protested: "No use looking at it that way. If
you want to clean up the lower courts, my method is
about the only one. The Vice Squad and the pigeons
frame the girls, and drag 'em into court. The girl, if
she can muster anywhere from fifty to five hundred
dollars, pays it over to some shyster in on the racket,
and he arranges a bail bond for her. He talks
to the magistrate, who lets her off for lack of evidence,
or something phoney. The magistrate, the lawyer, the
dicks and the pigeons split the money. The pigeon's
cut is usually ten dollars, sometimes fifteen or twenty."

"But—but for ten dollars these men—Oh, that's
horrible!"

Dan shrugged. "Well, at ten dollars apiece, and
they nab a lot of them, it mounts up. The dirtiest phase
of the thing is this: Once a girl has been arrested, they
convict her—innocent or guilty—if she won't come
across with the hush money. They work up a lot of
fake evidence against her. Bedford Reformatory and

the city jails are full of girls who've been framed because they wouldn't—or couldn't—pay."

"This is more horrible than corruption in office, or graft!"

"Then use a stool pigeon. I'm sure I can lay my hands on a few of them. But there're two that know more than the rest. One of 'em is called The Swan, God knows why. The other is a South American called Panama Gomez. Either one will talk for money. What do you say?"

The Colonel sighed. Dan saw he was oppressed by the muck that was being turned up. Then the older man nodded heavily. "I don't like it, but if necessary, we will do it."

Dan got up to go before he changed his mind. "Well, you let me know as soon as you hear from Adams about Martineau. Then I'll go to work."

He left the Colonel.

He had dinner in a downtown speakeasy—laid in a heavy groundwork of vegetable soup, sirloin steak with potatoes and string beans, and then coffee. He had told Portis a lot, but he hadn't told him that tonight he was attending the opening of Lila Bennett's new place, where the Mayor of New York would be. He hadn't told him either that the Mayor had a finger in the backing, as Firenze was ostensibly part owner with Lila. Dan was going that night, and that would be the first time he would see Lila in what was now months.

He stopped in the Berlin and got into dress clothes, putting away three straight scotches meanwhile. By eleven he felt pretty well, and hopped off in a cab for the new place, only around the corner from the old, in Fifty-second Street, East.

Leaving his hat and coat with the check girl, he wandered around. Only a few people he knew had arrived, and he gave the place a thorough inspection. He was growing very cautious since the night he had learned his Rosenberg list had been lifted. He found a back entrance through the kitchen, and another down through the cellar. Otherwise the layout conformed with most speakeasies on the East Side: entrance foyer, dining room in front served by French and Italian waiters, then a small barroom with a few tables around the walls. The ladies' and men's rooms gave off the bar. There were other and smaller rooms upstairs on the same order as Lila's old ones. One with a grand piano. On the third floor was Lila's private apartment.

Then Dan came face to face with Lila in the barroom. He smiled easily at her. "Hello!"

Her face became mask-like. "Why, Danny-boy! How have you been?"

"I been great, thanks. And busy."

"Oh, I know how it is! Well, glad to see you around again. What do you think of the place?"

"Great. Coming up in the world, aren't you?"

She shrugged smooth white shoulders. He experienced an almost poignant return of his old liking for her. "I still go for you."

She smiled coldly, showing her pointed-looking teeth. Then she left him to greet arriving guests. They poured in. None of the Hall master minds came, but Harding, with Helen on his arm, drifted in about twelve. It got noisy. Moses and Steinmetz, both big lawyers and pals of Harding, came in and stayed a while. Show business was there in force, and by one o'clock it was hectic and the opening was a success. For the special occasion, Lila put on a little show: a few nude dancers and some singers of risqué songs. After that, Dan found himself beside Lila.

She said, her eyes just looking at him: "I want to talk to you. I couldn't when Harding was here that time."

"Why not now?"

She glanced around briefly. Then she nodded and led the way upstairs to her own apartment. It was luxuriously furnished in black, silver, red and gray modern furniture, as had been the first. She said without preamble:

"We've got a lot to say to each other."

He sat down and smoked. "I haven't got anything special to say to you."

She laughed with a little hard catch in her voice. "Oh, no? I want an explanation, Dan. What about Pasquale?"

"I don't know anything about him. No more than you told me."

"Then how did De Angelis get hold of it? The list?" Her eyes glittered, and Dan understood she had been living in a deadly fear of him for the last ten months.

He took advantage of it and looked at her blankly. "I wouldn't know."

Her voice became throaty. "For God's sake, tell me! What are you thinking?"

"You ought to know." He leaned forward and put his elbows on his knees.

"Damn you! You think I spilled it!" Now it was out and she ran a hand over her black hair. "You think that, don't you? Well, it's not so!"

"All right."

"You don't believe me!"

"You're doing all the talking." There was a knock on the door. Firenze came in. Dan said: "Excuse you."

Firenze glared. "I can come in. I want to talk to Lila."

Dan said: "Talk to her."

Firenze stood still. Lila said: "You came in on an argument. Dan thinks I spilled to somebody that Pasquale was on the list."

Dan could have broken her neck for that. Firenze looked quickly at him. "So?"

Dan told her: "You're panicky. *You* said I thought

that. I didn't. Besides, I didn't know it then, and had nobody to tell it to."

"I say you did know it," Firenze snapped.

Dan stood up. "Oh, do you? Who asked you?"

"I'm telling you."

"Shut up!"

Lila stumbled: "Oh, cut it out! Let's forget it. Albert, I'm only kidding."

Firenze faced Dan foursquare. "Well, I'm not. I say Dan spilled that to somebody, either then or later. Tell me what you're doing going in and out of a building in Wall Street where Colonel Portis has his office."

Dan tensed. This was tougher than he had expected. "You're a lousy liar. If I do think Lila spilled it, that's my business and none of yours. Which reminds me, maybe you're not so lily-white in this affair."

"That so?" Firenze's lips snarled.

"Funny your married sister and De Angelis' sister are so pally. I often wondered about it."

"Meaning what?"

"Meaning maybe you tell things to your sister, and maybe she talks a lot too."

Firenze's eyes widened, then narrowed, all in a split second. "You rotten double-crosser!"

Lila cried: "Albert!"

Dan's teeth ground together. "Listen to me! I don't like you. I never did. One more word and I'll smack you."

"Cut it, you two!" Lila pleaded.

Firenze set his feet apart. "You'll do what?"

He wasn't set for the right hand jab that caught him on the side of the jaw. He reeled and went for his hip pocket. Dan started in with both fists. His left came down, raking the wop's face from top to bottom. Dan's knuckles hurt him. His temple buzzed from a stinging blow. His shoulder pained from another. He saw the glittering eyes in front of him and lashed out. Crack. The eyes were gone. He moved forward and brought his right to the side of the jaw again. He had weight and height advantage, and used it. Firenze was capitalizing on his stockiness and bull shoulders. Dan followed with a straight left, but the Italian, grabbing his arm, almost broke it.

Dan twisted and they spun around. He used his foot and sent the wop crashing to the floor. The back of his head hit and he lay stunned. Dan grabbed his coat front with his left hand and stood him up. The right again, twice. He broke the wop's nose, and two teeth went on the next one. The secretary to the Mayor snarled like an animal, and tried a kick at Dan's groin. It barely missed, but the pain came just the same. Dan raked from top to bottom again, and then put all his steam in a right to the button. The Italian went out cold.

He lay on the floor where Dan dropped him, his face a mess, his tuxedo front red with blood. Dan went into

the bathroom and washed his hands—he thought one
finger was broken. He took the blood off his own face,
and straightened his clothes. He went back in and
found Lila waiting for him. The wop lay still on the
floor.

"I'm going," he told her. "When he comes to, tell
him to—Oh, tell him anything you want!"

Lila's eyes glowed softly. It was clear that she admired Dan for having been able to whip Firenze, had
probably thought he couldn't do it, and now was all
hipped. "Danny, we can get things straight between
us," she murmured.

"Not if he owns this joint."

She approached him. "Let's—let's try."

He shook his head.

She said angrily: "You're poison to me, big boy.
But I like you."

"Safer for you not to. I'll be seeing you."

He went home and slept until two o'clock the next
afternoon.

CHAPTER XIII

The Hand of Jim White

THE wolves had had Pasquale thrown to them. Then on their own hook they got Brunner, his successor. They got others, four or five in all, and the public awoke to the sink-hole condition of many of the Magistrates' courts. It hadn't been necessary for Dan to do anything further along that line. State Senator De Groodt and his cohorts kept up a continual yelling for an inquiry, and the moment was approaching when Martineau might be appointed.

Suddenly, De Groodt sprang the threat of a city-wide inquiry, the idea being to put Governor Van Brunt Adams in a hole, since the Gubernatorial campaign was about to begin. The past two years had been replete with Republican Legislative efforts to put Adams in a hole—make him antagonize his own party, or a division of it, and the demand for a city-wide inquiry, coming at this time, was so intended. Ordinarily, there was nothing to worry about. The politics of it was too plain, but what plagued the insiders was the revelations growing out of the investigation of the courts by the Appellate Division, with particular reference to the manner in which various judges had bought their jobs. So there was nothing unusual in Tully's gathering of the clan at his home the night of August 23rd.

Dan wasn't called, but Quinn was of course supposed to sit in. Dan was about to leave the office when his phone rang.

"Dan, this is Mr. Quinn."

"Yes, sir?"

"I'm expected at Mr. Tully's tonight at eight, but I can't go. You'll have to go in my place."

"I don't know if they'll want that."

The querulous old voice wavered over the wire. "Well, it's impossible for me. I'm flat on my back with that bad liver of mine. The pain is awful. You go to represent me, and let me know in the morning what happened. I haven't been told what it's about."

Dan telephoned Betty and broke his date with her. He had dinner and went to Tully's, arriving at five minutes to eight. Dietrich and Calloway were there ahead of him. They chatted. Dolan, well-set up and Irish as hell, came and greeted them gruffly.

Dan told Tully: "Judge Quinn is sick with his liver. Asked me to sit in here for him tonight. I'll report to him in the morning."

Calloway remarked. "He's not a very healthy man, is he?"

"Look how old he is," Tully dropped.

Harding and Firenze came in with a sprightly swagger. By ten past eight they were all there. Dan saw, by the casual but mystified air they wore, that nobody knew what this session was about. Not a hint had been dropped, and now Tully seemed in no hurry. He said:

"What do you boys think of Brand's candidacy?"

Harding replied scornfully: "Where the hell can he get?"

Dietrich sounded cautious: "I'd like to know if Adams is going to pay any attention to De Groodt. A nuisance, that De Groodt."

"He's persistent," said Dan. De Groodt had been a tack on the Hall seat for years, and he grew sharper as time passed.

Tully smoked peacefully: "I doubt if Brand has any ammunition that means anything. You'll see Adams re-elected."

"If Brand stays dry, he'll never carry New York, or any city."

Dietrich jeered: "Dry! He'll climb on the wet wagon before long. He's not such a fool as to let the Republican drys make a set-up of him, as they did with Boerum and Wagstaff in the campaigns against Jim White. But Brand really hopes to win on the basis of scandal."

Harding laughed loudly. Dan wondered what they were waiting for. Certainly Tully wasn't going to waste an evening discussing Brand's running for Governor. Something big was brewing.

"What about Brunner?" Calloway asked of Tully, who shrugged.

Harding replied: "We don't know anything about him. Maybe we can get him off, though." Tully shook his head to that.

A peculiar silence of suspense gripped them all, and they sat and smoked. Nobody had said they were waiting for anything, but they all waited, obviously, without knowing for what.

An end came to it when Jim White arrived. Harding was so surprised at this that he goggled. Dan saw Calloway and Dietrich exchange a brief glance, without meaning for the young lawyer, though he could guess that Tully had taken this secretive method of getting them together to prevent any advance master-minding being done. It worked. Everybody was surprised.

White came in briskly, and beyond his business-like greeting he made no attempt to be cordial. Tully's thin lips twitched in a covert smile of triumph at his little strategy. He said:

"Take a seat, Jim. Let's get right down to business."

"You bet," answered the ex-Governor. "I've got quite a story to tell you fellas, and you better listen hard. I've been up to Albany this morning and talked to Adams."

"Well?" Dietrich leaned forward.

White swept them all with a glance. "He was considering this business of the inquiry. The question was what to do about De Groodt."

Harding said: "Aw, why bother about him? He's a lot of wind, and it's just a political trick."

White looked at the Mayor, smoke from his cigar veiling his eyes. "It is politics, and pretty clumsy at that, but it's got to be taken seriously because of this row coming here. I told Adams to ignore the matter."

"He can't ignore it altogether, Jim," Tully said.

"No, not entirely. But they can't make politics out of his refusal to have an inquiry now. City-wide means a pretty drastic affair, and it's expensive. Nothing has happened to justify Adams going as far as that. But there's a bigger reason which won't be in the papers tomorrow, when he makes his reply to De Groodt and the rest of the Republicans."

Harding moved in his seat. Dan understood the uneasiness he felt at White's slow return to power. Adams had crossed them all by going to the defeated Presidential candidate for his advice rather than to them. This gave White a great measure of power that he would not have had as a mere Hall sachem. When it came to big-time State and city politics, they were going to be forced to admit the superior political sense of White. He went on:

"The point is that Adams must be reëlected, and he's not going to win votes by turning against his own party now. He knows and we all know that New York City will go with him because he's got a good record and because he's a wet. Up-state ought to go with him because of his stand on water power." This last, Dan knew, was motivated by White's long ambition while a Governor himself. "Adams won't win votes by starting to rake up a lot of dirt in his own party, even if he's not a close inside Hall man. Besides, this election has got to be kept to State issues. Political scandal and corruption in office is local, that's all."

Tully: "That's right, it strikes me now. Brand will make most of his campaign on the dirt, or what he thinks he can lay his hands on."

White pointed a finger. "Now, that's the angle. Brand is dry-ish now, but I think he'll try to straddle the fence later, in order to hold his up-State Republican drys, and in order to win some wet votes in the cities. I don't think he can lick Adams. Anyway, we're backing Adams, and at the moment it's got nothing to do with the city. He's dropping all idea of a city-wide inquiry, for the simple reason that nothing really important has come up. I think the organization here is safe."

Calloway leaned back in his seat. Dietrich lit a fresh cigar. Harding smoked fast, Firenze stared at the ceiling, and Dolan just sat there, taking it all in. That was all he could do, because he had inherited the Police Department from the bus-man, now again in the bus business, and he had his hands full. White flicked his cigar ash and did a little thinking. Then he said:

"I'm not finished yet. I've given you the State angle of the situation. But now I have another point: I make no secret of the fact that unless we're all very careful, the Hall is going to suffer before the next Mayoralty campaign comes around. Now, I'm going to talk straight out."

The air of suspense returned.

"The Mayor of New York has got to behave himself personally. Wait a minute. I'm not through."

Harding killed his cigarette. Firenze didn't look at the ceiling now. Every pair of eyes in the room was fastened on White. The political mentor continued, talking emphatically.

"Five years ago I gave my support to William Harding, then a State Senator, because we all believed that he had the power to capture the public imagination, and because he was the acceptable kind of man to get rid of the previous régime. All that we know about and understand. But none of us foresaw—I'm speaking right out and it's important—that the Mayor would make a public spectacle of himself. Mind you, I don't object to him being a good guy. That's great and is worth lots of votes. But too much gossip has been getting around. It makes us all ridiculous."

Harding gnawed at his lower lip.

"Now I know what somebody's going to say. If I

felt this way, why did I give my support to his renomination last year? For manifest reasons." He looked
at Tully. "I'm going into all this just to show you I'm
not flyin' off the handle." He faced the rest again. "If
I hadn't backed Harding, it coulda been said that I
was flighty. It coulda been asked what had the Mayor
done behind the scenes that made me object to him,
when I approved him four years before? Awkward, that
woulda been. Now, he hasn't steadied down any. Get
this. I'm not talking only about the Hall. Don't forget
the Hall is only part of the Democratic Party in the
State, and the Mayor of New York City is making the
Democracy ridiculous north of the Bronx. How can we
build up a man like Adams when this other man is act-
ing like a fool?"

Harding jumped. "You've got a damned nerve!"

White was growing angrier. "You sit down. You're
to take orders, but I guess you don't even know how to
do that." He stood up himself. "Nobody cares if you
chase every girl in the city, but it's not necessary to do
it publicly. That's the point! Let's go back a couple of
years. When I was running for President, the Republican papers published rumors that you were goin'
to be my Secretary of State, if I was elected. That
was goddam nonsense, but what could I say? It made us
all look like a pack of fools, because you're a joke!"

Harding forgot to bluster and spoke in a fury:
"Where in hell would the lousy Party be if I wasn't

around to get votes for you? Don't talk to me like that!"

White's voice grew louder: "I'll tell you what's orders! You've got to behave yourself!"

Harding ground out: "Mention one thing you object to."

"I object to a certain place being known, almost publicly, as the Mayor's Speakeasy."

Harding literally snarled, without getting any words out.

"Now, understand. I forbid you to go there any more!"

"You'll forbid me nothing," yelled Harding. "I'll do what I goddam please. Get that, you big stiff!"

White lost his temper. He was on Harding like a tiger, both hands at the Mayor's throat. Everybody stood up. White, though the older man, forced him with a crash against the wall, where Billy's head thudded. White banged the head from side to side, hitting the wall each time.

"You tin-horn politician! We'll get some sense into your head, if we have to open it up! You'll take orders, or get kicked out! By God, I—" His flare of rage went as swiftly as it had come. He took his hands away. Harding gasped, his eyes bulging. Everybody sat down, ever so quietly, watching White, who returned to his chair.

From there he said to Harding: "That's an order."

"To hell with you!"

Dan thought it would start again, but White relaxed in his chair. He spoke to them all: "I'm sorry that had to happen. We're past the stage of foolin' around like schoolboys."

Voices said all together, including Tully's: "I guess you're right, Jim." "Okay!" "Fair enough." Dietrich listened gravely.

Calloway asked: "Anything special we have to do, Jim?"

"No, nothing now. Except bear in mind what I've said."

Dan grinned to himself. A new master for the flock. Or rather, an old one back. Tully seemed relieved. Someone else was here to help with the responsibility.

They broke up, and it was hardly ten o'clock. Harding and Firenze went off in the sedan. Dan went to Lila's, after stopping in a restaurant for some food. Thinking made him hungry. Pancakes, syrup and two cups of coffee.

He found the place deserted between dinner and supper. He had Benny call her down from her apartment. She came down and smiled to him. They had a pair of drinks and sat at a table in the front room.

"We had excitement tonight, baby. They told Billy not to come here any more."

She looked at him with interest. "That so? Why?"

"It's called the Mayor's speakeasy, for one thing."

She lifted her upper lip in a grimace of scorn. "Oh, what of it?"

"I just thought I'd tell you."

"Thanks. But Billy will take care of it, I guess."

"Yeah."

The front bell rang and the headwaiter went to let two men in. They walked down the aisle between the table booths.

They recognized Dan, and he them.

"Hello, how are ya? What's up?"

One of them tipped his hat to Lila. "Sorry, Miss Bennett, we're raidin' the joint."

"What? Nobody told me about this!" She flashed a look at Dan, who sat tight, thinking fast. These were Federal men. One of them pulled out a warrant and showed it to her. "Where do ya keep y'r liquor?"

Lila got up and went into the barroom with them. One man in there was drinking. He finished his drink, but didn't pay for it and walked out. The bartender already had his apron off and was lounging, reading a paper.

He looked up. "H'lo, boys! Whad'll ya have?"

"H'lo, Benny. Didn't know you was workin' here."

"Oh, I just dropped in!" and he grinned.

The two men inspected the place, went behind the bar and took a half-pint of whisky for evidence. "Ya'll have ta come with us, Benny."

He sighed, went into a back room and in a few seconds emerged ready for the street. The taller of the two dicks said to Lila:

"You'll have ta show in court. Here's the summons."

She accepted the document, her face set in rigid anger. Dan said: "You don't need me," and walked out. Across the street he dove into a drug store telephone booth and called the Mayor.

"Billy, they just pinched Lila's place. Two Federal guys from the Prohibition unit."

"I'll be God-damned! That lousy bum White did that!"

"No, he didn't, Billy," Dan soothed. "He wouldn't do that. He expects you to take the hint. I think Dietrich or Calloway took it first. Quick work, anyway."

A pause, then— "Tell Lila I'll fix it up tomorrow."

"Okay. They'll probably rap her for a fine or something. They took Benny."

"Ta hell with Benny!"

Dan went back to Lila. The dicks were gone, and she was there alone, with the waiters, pacing the barroom. When he entered, she sat him down in a booth.

"You're a lousy double-crosser, Dan! What did you do that for?"

"What?"

"The raid. It'll cost me money to get Benny out. And me."

"I didn't do it. Somebody else did it."

She looked straight into his eyes. "I don't believe you."

"I just talked to Billy. He's going to fix it in the morning."

"That was neat of you."

"You could thank me."

"Thank you for trying to queer this and cost me a lot of money?"

He smoked without comment.

She leaned forward. "You did this because you still think I spilled the Pasquale dope." The gleam of fright was in her eyes.

He said: "That's what you think."

CHAPTER XIV

Commissioner Martineau Loosens the Lid

WHAT started on September 8th to be one of Dan's normal visits to Colonel Portis contained a surprise for him. The financier showed him to a seat, and said:

"I want you to wait with me for a few minutes. I am expecting a very important visitor whose acquaintance I desire you to make."

Dan waited.

"Judge Cullen Martineau."

Dan was alarmed. "He coming here?" The day before, the appointment of former Judge Martineau as Special Commissioner had been announced.

Dan stood up. "I'd rather not meet him. It's too dangerous."

"Dangerous? Why?"

"Dozen reasons. I'm in a hot enough spot now."

"I'm sorry. I hope nothing will happen. But I do want you to meet Judge Martineau. He's a wonderful man, as you know, and I—please sit down and wait for him. He should be here now."

Dan sat down. He didn't care for this at all. "Then,

don't tell him of—of our work. I'd be anxious to keep
that under cover."

"Very well. But I have told him a few things about
you. That you know New York politics extremely well,
and—"

The sexless secretary showed in a tall, massive man,
with iron-gray hair above a ruggedly determined face.
The expression of the eyes was clear and fearless. He
and Portis shook hands, and Portis introduced Dan to
him.

"I have heard of you, Mr. Fitzhugh," Martineau
said, as they all lit cigars. "Weren't you to have been
nominated for the Legislature a few years ago, and it
didn't come off?"

Dan was surprised. But then, perhaps Martineau had
heard of it from White or Walters. The Judge was a
prominent Democrat. "That's right, sir," he answered.

The steady, powerful voice of the jurist continued:
"And Colonel Portis has told me of you. He has spoken
very favorably."

"That's mighty decent of him." Dan kept waiting, to
make sure this was just a social visit. It soon turned out
not to be.

Martineau said: "I'm going to speak to the point and
frankly, because I know we're all busy men. You see,
Mr. Fitzhugh, I am of the personal conviction that the
Hall is temporarily finished as the ruling organization

in New York City. The courts are the least of it. That's what many of us think."

"You're entirely right. But I don't believe the Hall will go out of business."

"Oh, no! Its hold on the lower-class wards is too strong. But the present group of leaders—Harding, Tully, Calloway, and the rest—I believe that a new group will supersede them within the next few years. Perhaps even at the next Mayoralty elections. Don't you agree with me?"

Dan tried to master his amazement. He had known of Martineau a long time, but hadn't thought him to be such a hard-headed, "practical politics" sort of man. He replied: "I think you've got a better grasp of the situation than I have."

The noble head that many Democrats believed would some day grace the White House inclined itself in a small bow of thanks. "I have made that point, because it is necessary for the younger men interested in New York politics to realize that new leaders are coming in, for a time at least. That is why, in a large, general way, I would like to have your coöperation."

"My coöperation?"

"Exactly. Yours, and of other young men like you. While the process of undermining the power of the present Hall leaders is going on, the Democratic party must still be held together. The counsel of men like yourself will be invaluable to the independent Demo-

cratic leaders in advising, and in winning the support
of an organization that is built with practical politics
specifically in mind."

Dan felt a twinge of embarrassment. Here was Martineau, Special Commissioner of Governor Adams to
investigate conditions in the lower courts, asking his
political coöperation! No reason why he shouldn't extend it. He said so.

"I believe, also, Mr. Fitzhugh, that for men of your
ability there are good political careers ahead. Have
you thought of that?"

"Well, there was my nomination—"

The rugged face split in a smile. "Oh, I mean one
that goes through. Does that sort of thing interest
you?"

"Of course."

"Fine. Naturally you will not repeat this little conversation. We perhaps will not meet again for some
time. The investigation begins almost at once, as soon
as I have set up a staff. Furthermore, you will realize
that I must be very careful in all this, in order to avoid
accusations of political animus or ambition."

"They'll be made," said Dan bluntly.

Martineau spoke emphatically: "I intend to meet
them by conducting the investigation fairly!"

"Only thing to do." Dan found himself entertaining
an honest liking and admiration for the Special Commissioner. There was an impressiveness about him that

had to be met squarely. There was little use for evasions or innuendoes. Martineau added:

"I believe I have sufficient understanding of practical politics—to use that phrase again—to see that this investigation will not get far, or produce any appreciable results, unless it has some measure of public support. And it follows that public support, without some sort of a finger on the political pulse, is perfectly useless when it comes to elections. That is why I—"

Dan allowed himself a jot of enthusiasm: "There's one way to lick the Hall—or at least, give it an equal to fight, instead of the stupid Republican party here."

Martineau and Portis listened.

"It's the thing that every previous opposition to the Hall has always failed to do, God knows why. That is, start an organization just like it."

Martineau nodded at once, impressed. "Yes, but that takes time. Mr. Fitzhugh, clean blood is coming in at the next elections!"

"Yes, and it'll go after another four or eight years. It always has."

Martineau rose. Dan stood up and so did the Colonel. "When the old crowd have gone, Mr. Fitzhugh, we can talk about your idea. . . . I have enjoyed this talk very much."

Dan shook his hand warmly and left the two iron-gray heads. He entertained the vision of a political career—Dan was young yet—and he had a feeling

that Martineau was going to be a big man in the
political end of the State, though he was playing a
cleanly non-political hand now. Further, Dan knew that
Jim White approved of Martineau, personally and
politically, and if that didn't hint at the coming change
—what could?

Monday morning. Dan was in the Supreme Court,
prosecuting a murder case. Two amateur gunmen had
wounded a patrolman in trying to hold up a small
jewelry store on upper Broadway. Justice Kendall sat
on the case. Recess came and Dan, to his surprise, was
called into chambers by Kendall. He noticed the jurist's
scared eyes. They sat down in the small room back of
the bench and smoked. Luncheon was brought in for
them both in a few minutes.

Kendall said: "Say, Dan, I've been wanting to talk
to you."

"Now's your chance."

Kendall's little eyes roved. "It's sort of—sort of—
Listen, you'll have to keep it quiet."

"You'll have to tell me what it is."

The man couldn't look at him. "You've handled a
few little side jobs, haven't you?"

Dan tensed. "Meaning?"

"Well, I know you have Harding's confidence, and
Tully's, and I guess they—"

"I do 'em personal favors, if that's what you mean."

Kendall leaped at that. "Personal favors. That's it! I've got one I want you to do for me."

"Why?"

The man fidgeted and couldn't eat. "I—I'll make it worth your while, and—"

"Well, what is it?"

The judge looked at the door and lowered his voice. "I heard that there's copies of the Rosenberg list floating around."

Dan's throat went dry. That would be his list—his copy.

"Go ahead."

"Well, you know my name is on the God-damned thing, and I've got to get hold of it. Man alive—"

Dan felt a laugh inside himself. Was he going to be asked by every politician in New York to steal that infernal list? "I don't think you heard correctly. The only real copy is in Tully's hands."

Kendall got excited. "I heard it right, all right. Look at this." He fished in a pocket under his robe and brought out a long flat envelope. From that he took a stiff sheet of paper, folded lengthways. He handed it to Dan, who opened it.

He saw a photostat of what he recognized as one page of the Rosenberg list. It contained names and addresses of non-political individuals—dope, probably. He noticed that the tails of the t's and the lower curve of the e's were missing. His typewriter did that. This page had been photostated by whoever had lifted his list from the hotel safe. He sat up.

Kendall demanded: "That's it, all right. Now where is the original list? This is only a photograph." Beads of sweat stood on his forehead. "God, if that gets into Martineau's hands, I'm ruined!" His little eyes were round and his fat little cheeks quivered. Dan asked him:

"Where'd you get this? How'd you get it?"

"I was shown it."

"Who by?" Dan demanded impatiently.

Kendall hesitated. "Firenze."

Dan clamped his teeth together to prevent an exclamation. It had been Firenze who had stolen his list. "What did he tell you?"

Kendall looked around nervously. His fingers twiddled. Dan said: "Come on, spill the whole thing! I can't help you unless you do."

Kendall sighed and sank back. "All right. But you'll have to help me!"

"If I can! Think I can pull the list out of my hat?"

"Well, I went to Harding last week and told him Firenze should sell me a piece of good land he's got where the Seventy-fifth Street Bridge is going to be. I told him I'd have to have it. I was taking too much risk, passing on these condemnations, and unless I did, I'd make trouble. Hell, do they think I'm going to do a lot of the dirty work and then have that lousy Italian

get as big a share as me? Not on your God-damn' neck!
Harding said he'd find out. Next thing, Firenze drops
in on me with this photo of a page from the list. Said
he'd bought it from a gangster. The bastard hinted
that if I didn't shut up, he knew where to find the rest
of it. Now, you gotta get me the rest of it—the
original, and I'll stick a knife in that skunk's belly!"
Kendall was whiningly enraged. "I'll get that land
from him whether he likes it or not!"

Dan thought a long time. This pinned the theft on
Firenze, but of course he couldn't tell Kendall that.
Maybe he could get his own list from Firenze by force.
He came to a sudden decision: "Here. I don't think the
original is circulating. Tully had it, and he'll hold on
to it. They sent a phoney copy to Brand, and that can't
hurt you. Now, I'll find out, and maybe Firenze's just
throwing a scare into you on his own hook to shut you
up. I'll let you know."

Dan quit the mewling judge with pleasure. He walked
around the block for a breath of fresh air. He wouldn't
be sorry to see Kendall get it in the neck. They finished
up the case that afternoon, and Dan, right after he left
the court, went to Lila's.

She greeted him coldly. "I wish you wouldn't come
here. You've got a nerve."

"Still feel that way? Can't I drop in for a chat?"
He lit a cigarette. The bartender and waiters were the

only other people there. In a few minutes the dinner crowd would be in.

"I'm finished with you," she told him coldly. "Nobody can do me a dirty trick like that raid and get away with it."

"I told you I didn't have anything to do with it. You talk like a woman."

She flared: "You're a liar! I know damn' well you did it because you think I'm a double-crosser like you are!"

"Happy days are over. Who fixed up the raid?"

"Billy."

He took her hand in his. It was cold. "Take a hint. This joint'll be put away good one night and you won't have anything. They don't want this joint to run."

"You're getting dull."

"Have it your way. I'm telling you. Stop listening to that greasy wop and get some sense in your head."

She sneered with honest hate. "I liked you, Dan. But you're a—a—I hope somebody does for you!"

"Aw, baby!" He was considering her dispassionately. If she kept up this way, she was dangerous. Funny too, because a few nights ago, when he had given Firenze the beating-up, she had smiled on him. The wop had told her something about him. He got up to leave. "You won't be seeing me," and he left.

No use wasting time. Firenze was the poison in the dish, and the poison had to be eliminated. Dan ate dinner and then took a cab to the corner of Fifty-third Street and Tenth Avenue. He walked a block south, then half a block east. He went in a dark area-way door. A man in a dirty white shirt grunted and let him in. He went into a little dingy barroom, and spoke to the bartender:

"Anybody here?"

The man looked at him, beady-eyed. "Yeah. Louis is in the back room with Jack."

"I'm going in." Dan walked through a small door, and reached a small square room with two curtained and shuttered windows. A couple of men, well-dressed and sleek, sat at a table eating steaks. Glasses of beer stood by their plates.

"Hi, Dan!" one of them mumbled.

"Hey, there, Louis!" Dan sat down with them. The bartender came in. "Bring me a scotch." The bartender went out, and returned with a small cylinder brimming with amber. Dan drank it off.

"What're you boys up to these days?"

The men's pale faces sneered in disgust. "Nothin'. It's dull as hell. Say, Dan, who's gonna get in a jam over this inquiry?"

"None of you guys, I don't think. Just pigeons and cops and lawyers and magistrates."

"Them goddam pigeons stink, anyway," Jack said. "Hope they burn 'em."

"Maybe." Dan looked at Louis. "Hey, Jack, when

you finish, beat it. I want to talk a little business with Louis."

"Okay." Jack gulped down the last mouthful of steak, washed it down with beer, lit a cigarette, and went out. The other man took out a small cigar and watched Dan, who said:

"Busy tonight?"

"Nope."

"Ever hear of a friend of mine by the name of Albert Firenze? He's secretary to the Mayor."

"Yeah, I guess so."

Dan explained: "He runs a speak in Fifty-second Street. The Mayor's Speakeasy, they call it. He goes home around four in the morning, and he's careless. I'm always afraid he'll get hurt, he's so careless."

"Too bad."

"He's a little dark guy, with wide shoulders."

"I know what he looks like. I worked for him once or twice, downtown."

"Oh! Well, I'd hate it if he got hurt very badly to-night."

"Suppose you heard he was all set to be measured for a wooden kimono?"

For answer, Dan took out five hundred dollars in centuries, which Portis had paid him that Saturday afternoon. "Five more when you come back," he said.

Louis' face was a blank as he pocketed the money. "I'll be back about five, I guess."

"I'll wait. Here's the address." Dan printed it with a stub pencil on a piece of yellow paper. "Throw it away when you've read it."

The professional killer grinned and went out.

Dan sent for magazines and papers. He read, drank scotch and smoked. Nobody else came into the room, because he told the bartender not to allow any one. Time went slowly, and he grew sleepy. He tilted his chair back against the wall and napped. He shivered and woke up. It was two-forty. He slept again, and came to with a start when he heard voices in the front room. The door opened. Jack, Louis' pal, came in and stared at Dan. Then Jack disappeared.

He came right back with the bartender, and they supported between them a man, whom they laid down on the floor. He was bleeding from the mouth, and there was a large patch of blood on his waistcoat. It was Louis. He was already dead. The gun had failed to get the guy he had gone after, Jack admitted dispassionately. Instead, the guy had shot him.

"He jus' managed to crawl into the area-way here when he croaked," Jack said.

CHAPTER XV

Why a Judge Left Home

IT WAS on September 10th, two days after State
Supreme Court Justice Eugene Kendall disappeared,
like that, that the sexless secretary attached to Colonel
Portis' office came to see Dan at his hotel right after
dinner. He had his coat and vest off, and had been lying
on the bed, reading the newspaper speculations as to
why the Judge had taken it into his head to vanish.
Nobody thought he had been murdered, because it was
improbable. Only two papers voiced the suspicion that
the forthcoming Magistrates' Courts investigations
might be about to turn up something on Kendall, and
that he had thought it wiser to go away than to face
it out. But the reporters soft-pedaled that suspicion,
since clearly the Judge might merely have taken a quiet
little trip, and would return pronto to sue for libel.

Dan was as baffled as anybody, though his conjec-
tures were closer to the truth.

There was too much mystery for Dan's own comfort
in two situations: one was this disappearance of Kendall and its connection with the probably phoney attempt of Firenze to scare the Judge out of demanding a

bigger split on the bridge site graft. The second puzzle was the reason why Firenze seemingly made no effort to pin on Dan the attempt to bump him off. The day after the dead gun had been laid cold on the speakeasy floor, Dan had seen Harding, who, between triumphant snickers, had recounted how the Italian had vanquished a mysterious sniping ambush.

"It'll take some sharpshooting to get him, Dan," the Mayor had said.

And Dan had asked: "Who's behind it?"

Harding replied: "Albert thinks it's some downtown gangsters—his own section."

There it rested.

Miss Peabody, the People's Franchise secretary, who was sexless by reason of her angular appearance, her cold face and her spectacles, sat on the edge of the small arm chair and looked at Dan. He lounged across the bed. She said:

"Colonel Portis wants to know why Justice Kendall disappeared."

"Why does he have to know?"

"I can't tell you. That's all he said, and he seemed annoyed."

"He should be glad."

Her thin-lipped mouth twitched. "That's not the answer I came for. I'd much rather be home for my dinner."

"You don't like me, do you?"

She relapsed completely into her secretaryhood. "I was merely reminding you."

Dan threw himself back against the pillows stacked at the headboard. "You going right back to him?"

"I may telephone him, if you can tell me something important."

"How do you know if it's important or not?"

She shrugged. "I'll have to take your word for it. I really don't know anything about this."

He thought for a while. He killed his cigarette butt and lit a new one. He didn't know why Kendall had disappeared, or even if he actually was some place unknown to the insiders, if it came to that. He talked slowly:

"The only thing I can suggest now is that maybe the Judge was scared of the investigation."

She remarked in a more friendly tone: "I don't see why he should be. A judge, and all."

"Yeah. Well, if you tell that to the Colonel, he'll understand, I guess. You might say, also, that Kendall was perhaps frightened of an exposé of a deal over the site for the Seventy-fifth Street Bridge. But you can't prove any of that."

It struck him now that neither of those reasons, spoken aloud, adequately accounted for Kendall's rout. But he couldn't tell Portis that Firenze might have scared the Judge away with the Rosenberg list. Especially after Kendall had begged Dan to snitch it back.

That would bear looking into. The only way would be to find out from whom Firenze had bought that photostat of one page of the list, if he had, which was more than doubtful. But it was impossible to give that dope to the secretary. Besides, she wanted to go home for her dinner. Flatbush, he thought. He told her:

"That's all the low-down I've got now. Tell the Colonel I think Kendall did this on his own hook, and that he's really gone under cover. Here; get an earful of this. Promise him I'll dig up the whole dope for him sometime soon."

Dan had suddenly decided it would be to his own advantage to learn where the panicky jurist had gone—and why.

Portis' secretary stood up. Her thin lips were compressed, and Dan understood her shy discomfort at being alone with a man in a hotel room. He stood up, too. She said: "I'll tell the Colonel. Can it wait till morning?"

"Sure."

He showed her out. Then he got dressed again and went out. From a phone booth he called the speakeasy near Tenth Avenue where he had spent most of the night four days before. A husky voice answered him.

"Jack there? Let me talk to him. . . . Hello, Jack? Dan. Where can I get hold of Panama Gomez?"

"The pigeon?" asked a tight-lipped voice.

"Yeah."

"On'y joint I know where he hangs out is a speak in a Hunner 'n' 'Leventh Street, right near the El. Ya know the joint?"

"No. Give me the name and number."

"Wait a minute. . . . Here. Eight-ten. Second floor. It's a spig joint. Ya know Panama, doncha?"

"Yeah. Okay, Jack. G'by." Double click.

Dan took a cab to the corner of One Hundred and Eleventh Street and Morningside. Then he walked two blocks to number 810. Up two floors and knocked on the door. A swarthy man, all of five feet high, opened the door a crack. A gust of smoky, fetid air swept out, mingled with a cackle of voices.

"I want to see Panama Gomez."

"Who you?" The little man's face was dark.

Dan reached in suddenly, grabbed him by the shoulder and spun him round. The man kicked, and Dan cuffed him. The man was obedient. Dan walked in. The speakeasy was a dingy three-room apartment. The front room had three small tables covered with dirty white tablecloths. Next was the kitchen, whence came the odor like hot garbage. In back was the living quarters of the five-foot man, his fat wife who looked like an Indian, and a wizened female child. Dan looked around. From the corner, a man grinned at him: a small, dapper man with a certain greasy good-looks. He wore a tan suit, mauve shirt and tie, and on the chair beside him was a light gray felt hat. Dan walked over:

"H'lo, Panama!"

"Sit down, Mr. Fitzhugh." The little man spoke English carefully and precisely. "Have a drink?"

"None of this belly-wash, thanks. Come on with me. I want to talk to you."

The man's eyes shifted. "I'm waiting for some one."

"A broad?"

"Well—" He shrugged.

"The hell with that. This is important. Come on."

Gomez, the stool pigeon, whispered with the glaring proprietor and left with Dan. They went walking on Morningside Drive.

"Listen, Panama. There's no dough in this for you, but you can help the District Attorney's office on a little job, see?"

"I am always glad to be of assistance to the District Attorney."

"Yeah," said Dan, thinking of Gomez's living, won by framing girls on vice charges and splitting extorted fees with magistrates and crooked dicks. "You know Judge Kendall screwed out, don't you?"

"Sure, I know that."

"Well, maybe you've got a little dope you might want to tell me that would give us an idea—"

"What makes you think, Mr. Fitzhugh—"

"Cut it. All you have to do is keep your trap shut, and tell me one thing. Did Firenze buy anything from you recently?"

The man's face was an honest blank. "What would he buy?"

"A bunch of papers, for example. Come across."

The pigeon protested. "No kidding, I don't know anything about it. I don't have anything to do with that wop."

"Know much about him?"

The little man shrugged. "Oh, this and that! What's it all about?"

They walked three steps in silence. Then Dan said: "Got any ideas as to why Kendall left? You don't know if Firenze scared him out?"

"I'd know it if he did. I know all about the courts. You bet I'd know it. Kendall didn't leave for no reason like that. I know why he left."

Dan looked at him sideways. "You do like hell. Why?"

"He's mixed up with a lot of bum broads, see? Dames that get pinched on vice charges, and all, see? I think he got scared. That's what I think."

Dan kept his surprise hidden in silence. Kendall mixed up with underworld women! That didn't sound probable, since he had never heard 'a whisper about Kendall's private life. He said as much. Gomez insisted:

"You don't believe it, huh? Want to come with me now, and I'll show you?"

"Sure."

They walked downtown to a dingy cheap apartment building in One Hundred and Ninth Street between Central Park West and Manhattan Avenue. Gomez took him to a flat on the third floor. The elevator was run by a Negro hallboy, the car itself was lifted by a hand rope, dirty uncovered electric bulbs illuminated the corridors. The apartment doors were painted bilious green. The stool pigeon rang the bell gingerly, and it was opened by a girl. Her toneless voice said:

"H'lo, Panama! Come on in." They entered. The girl cast an appraising eye over Dan. She was small and beginning to get fat. Her dark brown hair was straight and uncombed. She led them into a tiny parlor, containing a cretonne-covered sofa, a player piano and two upright chairs. She lit a cigarette and stood looking at them, waiting.

Gomez smiled and became sociable. He went up to her and put one arm around her, facing Dan. She had on a cheap negligee, and through it Dan could see a wrinkled slip, suggesting sagging breasts. Gomez's hand dug caressingly into the bulge of flesh above her hips. "We just dropped in to say hello, baby. This is Mr. Fitzhugh."

The girl just looked at him. Then she asked: "Wanna drink? I gotta little gin, if ya c'n stand that." She took Gomez's hand and put it away from her.

The pigeon sat down.

Dan said: "No, thanks. Panama tells me you were a friend of Judge Kendall's?"

She flashed a beady look at the smiling South American. Then to Dan: "What of it?"

Dan pursed his lips. "Nothing of it. I'm just mentioning the fact. Happen to know where he went?"

Her voice had a throaty note of panic: "What're you, a dick?" She took a step backward. Her negligee fell open, giving Dan a view of black-silk-stockinged legs, and white flesh between that and the slip. She closed it negligently. He said:

"I'm from the D.A.'s office. But don't get scared. Nothing's happening. Sit down."

"This on the level?"

Panama tossed in: "Sure, kid. We're just visiting, see? Naturally we're interested in the Judge."

The girl said resentfully: "Well, I don't know where the old fool went. But he used to be free with his money."

"See him lately?"

Her brown stringy hair tossed when she shook her head. "No. Not for a coupla months, I guess. He phoned last week, but I was busy."

That was all she knew. Once again on the sidewalk, they taxied to a very similar apartment in Sixty-ninth Street between Columbus and Broadway. In the cab Gomez said: "Believe me now? I'll show you another one."

Dan experienced definite surprise at this angle on Kendall. They entered another apartment and found another girl, this one very thin and scrawny and poverty-stricken looking. She had on a black dress that Dan thought was taffeta. She was more friendly,

evidently feeling herself more able to take care of
Gomez.

They spread themselves on a divan and they had a
drink of bad gin. Through a door Dan could see the
edge of a white-painted double bed sagging in the
middle. The girl ogled him. Gomez said:

"Mr. Fitzhugh's from the D.A.'s office, see? That's
his job, as if he was an auto salesman, understand?"

The girl's eyes hardened. "That's interestin'."

"We're just visiting around," Dan said. "Happen
to know Judge Kendall?"

Like the first girl, this one flashed a look of suspicion
at Gomez who smiled. Then she shot at Dan:

"Quit kiddin'. What's this about?"

Gomez explained. "We just want a little information, baby, that's all. Don't be scared. We just want
to know if you knew the Judge very well, and all that."

"Maybe."

Gomez's face menaced her. "Can it. I know he used
to come here overnight. Come across."

She inspected him. Then she said to Dan: "That's
right. Kendall used to drop in to see me every once in a
while. Nice guy, I thought. Owes me some dough,
though."

"See him lately?" Dan asked, grinning. This was a
hell of a way to spend an evening, but it was fun.

She shook her crow-like head. "Naw. Him 'n' me had
a fight one night. He got sick 'n' I didn't like it."

Then she ran dry, and they left. Gomez cackled in satisfaction. "Want more?"

"We haven't learned anything yet. Got more?"

The Latin bobbed his head. "Four or five, I guess. Sure I got more. Let's see, now."

They went to a slightly better place, a hotel on Broadway near Columbus Circle. In a large, airy room on the tenth floor looking toward the Hudson River over a bunch of black factory stacks, they found still a different girl.

"H'lo, Panama! What do you want?"

She wore black pajamas of cheap silk that clung to a good figure, indicating hips, stomach and breasts. She had black eyes and shiny black hair. Her lips were thick and wet, and her voice husky from gin and cigarettes. Against the black pajamas, Dan noticed how white her neck looked. They sat down and had a bumper of gin.

Panama told her: "We're visiting round tonight. I told Dan I'd have him meet some swell girls."

She smiled at Dan and her hand caressed her side. Dan said: "Just floating around. Suppose I want to call you up sometime, what's your name?"

"Maria."

"Maria what?"

"Maria Blake. Call me up any time."

"I might do that." He got up to extinguish his cigarette in an ash tray he saw on the bureau and found himself looking at a four-by-six photograph in a green leather propped-up frame. It showed a man and a girl against a tree. He looked more carefully and recognized Judge Kendall and Maria Blake. This was warm. He turned around.

"I see you're a friend of Judge Kendall."

The girl got up and walked sinuously over to him. She looked at him and at the photograph. "Yeah. I knew him." Her lips faintly suggested a baring of teeth.

"What's the matter?" he asked. Gomez sat still and watched.

She gestured with a strong white hand. "Hell, he was a good friend of mine and he ran out on me!"

"Guys like that always run out."

She raised fleshy shoulders. "Sure, they do. But what burns me is he didn't take me with him."

Dan took a chance, casually. "Oh, did he take somebody else?"

He got a sultry look from the black eyes. "You bet your neck. He took Cissie Lucas with him. You know her, Panama. She lives—lived—here with me."

Dan walked over and sat down again. "Well, what in hell made him beat it like that? Did he fall for this Cissie?"

"You wanta know an awful lot, doncha?" She was getting wary.

"I'm curious."

Gomez: "Go on, Maria. What can you lose?"

She laughed without mirth. "Well, he was up here one night, talkin' funny. I guess he was worried about somebody findin' him out, or something like that. I don't know."

"You mean he was afraid the investigation would get him?"

"Maybe that was it. I don't know, really. But I hope somebody gets him, runnin' out that way on me." Her pride was talking.

Panama laughed: "What do you expect, baby, when you monkey around with a man like that?"

"I don't expect to get left sitting on my tail!"

"Where did he go?" Dan asked.

"Havana." Then she bit her lip. "You're after him. Listen, you leave me out of this."

Dan stood up. "All I wanted to know is where he went." He crossed to her, leaned over and kissed her lips. She bit his lip, delicately. He straightened up. "I'll come and see you some time. I got business to do now."

"Listen, you leave me out of this."

Gomez said loudly as they walked out: "Sure we will, baby, sure we will. Good night."

In the street again, Dan said: "Well, he wasn't much scared of the inquiry."

"Let me tell you. There's this you don't know. I don't know it either, but I think it. I think she was stinging him for money on account of that photograph."

"That so?"

"Yes. He got scared. That's all. Could the inquiry get him?"

"Not for a long time. Maybe never."

"There you are."

Dan said as they walked downtown toward his hotel: "Wonder if that's on the level that he skipped to Cuba?"

Gomez thought a while. "I know a way we can find out. I got friends down there. Come on."

"I appreciate your doing this. Tomorrow I'll give you a century."

"I'm glad to do the D.A.'s office a favor. But I'll take the century, all right." And he laughed loudly.

"What are you going to do?"

"Send a cable. We'll find out if Judge Kendall is really there."

Dan considered. "Listen. You send the cable. Let me know tomorrow if it says yes or no, see? I'm going home now."

"Good-night, Mr. Fitzhugh."

"Oh, say, give me your address."

"You can always get me where you found me tonight."

"Okay. So long."

In the morning Dan got up early, telephoning Portis from a near-by drugstore.

Then, in clipped sentences, he told Portis the story of the night before, of the three girls and the photograph. He satisfied the old gentleman that Kendall, though it looked like it, had not run away from the investigation, accurately speaking. Blackmail was more like it. Portis said: "Do you think that will be found out?"

"I doubt it."

"Where did he go? Did you learn that?"

"No."

"That's too bad."

"Maybe somebody will find him."

They hung up.

During the day, Gomez telephoned him at the office. He said:

"My friend wires that he is there in Havana, with the girl, C. L."

"Great. Keep it under your hat. When I see you, I'll have a present for you."

"I am always glad to do a favor—"

"Yeah, I know. So long, and thanks."

Well, let them all wonder where Kendall went. Dan knew.

CHAPTER XVI

The Squealing of a Rat

THE morning of November 11th, Dan arrived in his office about ten o'clock. The day before, he had finished up presenting a case to the Grand Jury, and he had now withdrawn to allow that body to deliberate on his request for the return of an indictment of second degree murder on a homicide charge. He looked over the assortment of briefs, memos from Quinn, phone messages from the day before, when his own instrument buzzed. It was Miss Peabody.

"Will you telephone me in half an hour and I will give you some information?" This was his standard way of hearing from Portis.

"Right."

In twenty minutes, he went out and called from a booth. Portis' voice said:

"Of course you know that The Swan has disappeared?"

The morning papers had featured the vanishing of The Swan, as a certain stool pigeon was known. Dan, a month before, had induced The Swan to testify before Martineau in relation to the Magistrates'

Courts. The Swan had begun by describing the methods by which women had been framed on vice charges. Now he was gone. Dan said:

"He got scared, I guess, or else somebody drove him away."

"What can be done? Judge Martineau has had to suspend the inquiry today, owing to lack of this witness. He will spend the time in examination of some of the people mentioned by The Swan—lawyers, court clerks, bondsmen, and so forth. Have you any plan?"

"I'll dig you up another bird," Dan told him.

He called his office, informed the operator he would be out for a while, but would phone later, and started for One Hundred and Eleventh Street to find Gomez, whom he had not seen this four days after Kendall's disappearance, when he had handed the pigeon a hundred-dollar bill for his services. Insiders and outsiders were still baffled by the protracted hiding-out of the jurist.

Dan first got out his own new coupé—Portis' money had bought it. He drove to the spig speakeasy and this time, without difficulty, the sullen owner admitted him. Dan walked into the front room. There was nobody there. By now it was near twelve o'clock.

Dan asked: "Panama Gomez here? Or when do you expect him?"

The man shrugged.

"Come on, tell me. I'm a policeman, understand!"

The little shifty eyes focused in fright. The booze-
seller grew voluble. "No, I don' know where he ees.
I try fin' him for you. Ju' seet down. Have a dreenk?"
He grinned and showed brown teeth.

Dan had some red wine and lolled in a corner to
wait. This was going to be dull, but it was the only
way. He heard the man's voice in the other room making a lot of telephone calls, in broken English and
rattling Spanish. It went on for half an hour. Finally,
the speakeasy proprietor returned.

"I no can fin' heem, sir. You 'ave lunch, eh, an' I
try later?"

Dan nodded. He ate vegetable soup, beans, fish,
lamb and rice, finishing off with an orange and a cup
of gritty coffee. It was then a quarter past one. The
man went to the phone again and seemingly started
on the same round of phone numbers—girls' apart-
ments, Dan guessed. The man came in again.

"I leave message, eh? An'—" The phone rang and
he bustled out, to return after an excited conversation.
"That was heem. He coming in thirty minutes. Good,
no?"

Dan sighed and waited. The ash tray was full of
small butts by the time Gomez arrived, sweating.

"Ah, Mr. Fitzhugh, I am terribly sorry to have kept
you waiting so long. I was far downtown."

"I'm sick of this joint. But I've got a little business
to talk over with you. Sit down."

Gomez sat and ordered something to drink. A bottle of red wine was placed before them. They both drank. "I am always glad to do a favor for the District Attorney's office."

"Well, here's your chance to do another one," Dan told him. "What do you think of The Swan?"

Gomez's face tightened. He shrugged and said nothing. Dan said bluntly: "I want you to take his place."

The South American cried excitedly: "Say, do you think I'm crazy? I'd last about two minutes talking that way! I'm always glad to—"

"Cut it out. I know that speech by heart. Listen to me. You won't get in any trouble. All you have to do is tell Judge Martineau how you guys work your racket, understand?"

Gomez shook his head determinedly. "I'm getting along fine now. Why should I go and tell all that and get a lot of my friends in trouble?"

Dan saw he had to go to work. "Sure, I know. But here's the point. If you don't do it, I'll find somebody else. There's a thousand dollars down to start with." Gomez listened more attentively. Dan could almost see the Latin's mind working furiously. "And besides, if somebody else starts to talk, it's going to queer your racket, anyway. That's so, isn't it?"

"I don't think so. They still will have to pinch girls, and the only way is to frame them, see?"

"All right. Have that your own way, but it's going

to make it tough for a long time. Those few cops you guys worked with are going to quit taking chances, once some of them get sent down. And that's going to happen."

Gomez said and did nothing.

Dan continued, leaning over the table. "Now, figure it this way. It's going to be spilled, either now or later, by somebody. Maybe they'll find The Swan and drag him back. If not, they'll get somebody else. Now, why shouldn't you be the one to earn the money?"

"I'd like to stay alive," said Gomez doubtfully. The idea of large cash was getting him.

"And there's another angle still. You start to talk and your name'll be on the front page every day. That's publicity, boy. You'll be famous." The man's eyes glittered. "The tabs'll pay you for your life story —you know, every day you tell 'em something, and you'll get a few grand out of that."

"Sure, that all sounds great, but how do I know I'm not going to get bumped the minute I start to talk. Say, there's plenty I can tell!"

"Sure there is," Dan said softly. "And think of it. I can give you a grand today—at least, I'll arrange for you to get it, because a friend of mine is anxious to get hold of you. Then, in a few days, you'll get more, and then will come the dough from some newspaper. Your name, your picture—boy, I advise you to grab the chance!"

Gomez thought a long time. His face changed in expression from cupidity to fear, from self-satisfaction to doubt. He said: "I want to be sure I am not going to get shot. Police-guard, or something."

"That's easy. They'll not risk losing you. You'll have an armed guard all the time."

"Have another glass of wine." Gomez poured out the two glasses. Then his eyes gleamed suddenly. "Say, what have you got to do with this?"

Dan answered: "I told you. A friend of mine who's hooked up with the inquiry wants somebody to take The Swan's place. He knew I knew you."

Gomez was not convinced.

Dan said: "Well, I'm not worried about that, if you're not. What do you say? Better grab the chance."

Gomez thought some more, looking at Dan and then away again, until he said: "I'll do it. Give me the grand."

"Come on. I'll have to stop and get it."

They paid for the wine and went out. Gomez said: "Maybe the papers won't be interested."

"Oh, yes, they will!"

Gomez took a cab to Dan's hotel, Dan following closely in his own car. He saw Gomez get out and enter the lobby. He parked, went to the safe, observing Gomez sitting in a chair in a corner. He took from the safe a large thick envelope, containing cash. With that he went to his room, extracted a thousand dollars, resealed the envelope, came downstairs again, put away the envelope and went out. Gomez followed. Dan waited right by the door, and he dropped from the side of his mouth: "Bankers' Building, Broad Street."

Gomez climbed in a cab and Dan followed. They met again in the gold-and-gilt lobby of the Bankers' Building. On the eleventh floor Louis A. Wurstling, counsel for Special Commissioner Martineau, had his offices. It was now nearing five o'clock. Dan told the pigeon, as he handed him the envelope:

"See Wurstling. Tell him you want to spill your story. Tell him your conscience hurts you and you have to tell what you know. Got it?"

Gomez nodded.

Dan said: "And listen, if you get it in your head to talk about me, I'll know it quick enough."

Panama watched him glassily.

"Never mind what you think. Just don't talk."

The rat studied him, then nodded and disappeared in an elevator.

The morning of November 26th, some two weeks later, Gomez went on the stand and admitted framing over a hundred women in the course of his career as a stool pigeon, working with certain dishonest members of the Vice Squad. He named lawyers, policemen, court clerks and bail bondsmen, and hinted at magistrates. Wurstling got out of him more, perhaps, than he had intended to tell, but in one day Panama Gomez was becoming famous.

It was just before lunch that Dan, looking out of his private office door, saw Tom Tully pass on his way to Quinn's office. Three quarters of an hour went by. Dan grew hungry, but waited. He was rewarded at length. Quinn's office door was a few feet away, and the outer office was quiet because most of the staff was lunching. Dan heard Tully's voice:

"We'd better talk this over some more." The tone suggested baffled fury.

Quinn said mildly: "Very well. Tonight, perhaps. I am not entirely clear . . ."

Tully didn't answer. Dan walked out of his office and almost bumped into him. Tully looked at him, and without a word turned and entered Dan's office. His face was cold and angry.

Dan walked in after him, shutting the door. Tully threw himself into a chair.

Tully glared and asked: "How *do* you work for him?"

Dan sat down and said nothing.

Tully continued: "See what that stool pigeon said this morning?"

"I read about it. Looks tough."

"Tough! I tell you it's damned serious. I thought we had a way to ease it off, but that Quinn—my God!"

"What's the matter with him?" He saw Tully had to talk about it, or bust.

Tully bit off the tip of a thick cigar. "He doesn't even realize it's serious. Too bad, he says, and that's all. I want him to offer Wurstling an Assistant District Attorney's appointment to investigate the courts. He says he can't see the point of doing that."

"Maybe you'd have a chance then to smooth it down a little, you mean? Strikes me as a good idea." It was.

"Certainly it's good. Not only that, but we'd know what the hell Wurstling was going to do. This way he can spring anything, and he's too damned smart for comfort."

"One of the smartest there is, Tom. Suppose you let me talk to Judge Quinn. He listens to me."

Tully inspected him critically, with a new light in his eyes. "That's a good idea. He likes you. Think you can do it?"

"I can try. I'll talk to him after lunch. Or maybe he'll want to talk it over with me anyway. I give him a lot of advice."

Tully stood up. "Good boy. Go to it. Let me know tonight. I'll be home." He left.

That afternoon, by the comparatively simple argument that it showed the willingness of the District Attorney's office to coöperate, Dan gained Judge Quinn's consent. He sat in the office while the District Attorney offered Louis A. Wurstling the post of Special Assistant District Attorney to investigate the Magistrates' Courts. Quinn placed the rough copy in his pocket to show Tully that night or within a few days. He shook his head dolefully and went home, one hand pressing the spot where his liver was.

Dan, on the way to the Berlin, bought all the papers to read of Panama Gomez's first day's testimony. He read them before eating alone, and contained in the report was a list of the names of girls the pigeon had at one time or another framed. The names included that of Maria Blake, deserted girl friend of Supreme Court Justice Kendall. The report said that the court would want to question some of these girls. He wondered if Maria would be smart enough to move to New Jersey. He had a certain regard for her, because she had given him the information leading to the discovery of Kendall's whereabouts.

He went to bed fairly early, and was awakened by the insistent ringing of his phone.

"Headquarters calling."

"Go ahead."

"Girl been murdered in the Hotel California, near Columbus Circle. Coming over?"

"Certainly. Be there in twenty minutes."

Dan dressed swiftly, though this sort of call was nothing unusual. A representative of the D.A.'s office, Homicide Division, had to attend the scene of all

murders and suspicious deaths. In a few minutes, after
bolting a cup of coffee in a lunch counter on the corner,
he was taxiing to the Hotel California. This was the
hotel where Maria Blake lived.

In the lobby he found a uniformed patrolman, who
told him the room number: 1012. Maria Blake's room.
Dan hustled into the elevator, and went to the room.
There already he found the Medical Examiner, the
police stenographer, police photographer and two men
from the Homicide Squad. A patrolman stood by the
window. The room was gray with flashlight smoke. On
the floor beside the bed was Maria Blake, in the same
black pajamas. The jacket was torn open, apparently
in a struggle, exposing her bosom, which was covered
with blood.

Dan greeted the detectives.

"Five shots in her from a thirty-eight," one of them
said.

"Got any ideas?"

The bull-necked man shrugged. "Prob'ly some hook-
up with her name gettin' mentioned this morning. Anyway, she's through."

Dan used the phone to call his office, where certain
people were always on call. He had them send up a
stenographer for his report.

Reporters and news photographers arrived and were
not allowed in. They stood in the hall and took pictures
as people came and went. The detectives had in the

manager, the night manager, the house detective and elevator boys, and found only that two men, whom nobody was able to describe accurately, had visited the girl early in the evening. How long they had stayed, or how they had escaped, no one could tell. The rooms on either side were unoccupied, and there had been little chance of anyone's hearing the shots. Particularly as the Medical Examiner found in the girl's wounds flakes of white material, as if the gun had been muffled with a bath towel. In the bathroom they found a bullet-riddled towel plentifully stained with blood. There were few other clews.

A man came in, announcing himself as one of Mr. Wurstling's legal assistants in the inquiry. Both detectives volunteered little help.

"There's the gal," said one. "Figure it out yourself."

The lawyer, a little nauseated at the view of the distorted body, said sharply: "I think somebody could tell me who she is, and if there's any idea as to why she was killed."

Dan moved over toward the bureau. The photograph was still in its place, and no one had yet noticed it closely, probably because no one there knew what Kendall had looked like. The police photographer, punctuating his work with flashes, was still engaged in shooting the body from different angles.

The other detective said: "We don't know why she was killed."

The lawyer forgot them and made notes on an envelope. Dan wanted to grin. He now had his back to the bureau, which was out of line of the door. The two detectives were standing beside Wurstling's assistant, looking down at the girl. The patrolman was staring out of the window, and the stenographer and Medical Examiner were conferring in a corner by the telephone table. Dan reached behind him and slipped the photograph into his pocket. He lit a cigarette, and, when his own stenographer came, he dictated a routine report.

They all stayed until around five A. M., examining everybody in the hotel who might know anything. The manager and several others were held as material witnesses. They left a patrolman on guard and went home.

Dan reasoned that friends of Kendall, knowing she had been trying to pin blackmail on the Judge, had done her in, now that she was suddenly come into the limelight. But they had overlooked the photograph. Dan was satisfied to keep that angle of the situation, which few people knew, to himself. It would not help to have the Kendall case blow up now, simply because it would detract attention from the Magistrates' Courts inquiry. This would do no good.

Dan thought about the girl. She had been a good kid in her way. But Gomez had done for her, indirectly, by bringing her name into his list of framed women. Dan had brought Gomez forth. Viewed in this light,

Dan was suddenly struck with the connection—that in a very indirect way, by spilling what he knew, he had caused this murder. He laughed at himself for getting soft. Maybe he was just tired and disgusted. Whatever it was, he said to himself:

"I'm a stool pigeon myself!"

CHAPTER XVII

The Inside of a Bank Crash

FOR a long time things went smoothly for Dan, with little happening out of the routine. He kept in touch with Portis, but for the moment there were no important tasks for Dan. Gomez continued to testify, revamping his testimony several times, but in the main causing such an uproar that several magistrates were either called on the stand and had the courage to face it out, or else resigned under fire. Connie Dolan had to make public announcement that the Police Department had given up the stool pigeon method of making arrests under the vice laws.

Brunner, Magistrate Pasquale's successor, had resigned after a long fuss involving everybody from Harding down. The case had finally been dismissed, but Brunner had been nailed and forced out anyway. It had been necessary, however, for Governor Adams to show his hand to induce the Hall leaders and district bosses to waive their legal immunity as public officials before they would allow themselves to be questioned. Harding and Quinn had testified. In all, the situation had not been serious, since nobody worried much about Brunner. Quite honestly, the Mayor and the District Attorney had been able to say that they knew absolutely nothing about the machinations leading up to Brunner's appointment.

Meanwhile, in December, at the low water mark of financial depression, the Bank of the Empire State crashed, closing its doors suddenly on the public in all its more than fifty branches scattered through the city. The outcry was terrific, involving the State Banking Department, great financiers, legal lights and political executives. Revised banking laws at once became an issue in the State Legislature, and the Bank of the Empire State depositors organized themselves in a body to force an investigation of the institution, the payment of a fair percentage on the dollar, and perhaps a reorganization.

Betty de la Roche, Dan's little friend, met him one night after dinner at her apartment. He waited for her in the lobby, and together they went upstairs. She had just been to a meeting of the depositors, and told Dan:

"You ought to see the people there, Danny. Poor old women, chorus girls, hoofers, ditch-diggers—God knows what—all looking pale and worried. I hope they get that dirty bunch of crooks that's responsible. Do you think they will?"

"Oh, yes! Somebody'll be nailed to the mast all right."

She hung up her hat and coat in the closet and mixed a pair of highballs. Her wide eyes looked at Dan. He liked her a lot. "I lost every nickel I had, Dan."

"That's tough, kiddo. Why in hell didn't you tell me before?"

Her lower lip went out. "Why should I? That's my own trouble, I guess." Her eyes filled with tears. "Well, I haven't got anything now."

"I thought they arranged so you could borrow up to fifty percent of the amount of your deposit." He swallowed some of his drink.

She tossed her head, as if to drive away the tears. "Oh, what good is that? I owed that much! And there's so much red tape, it would take weeks to get it."

He moved closer to her and took her hand in his. She leaned against him. "Listen, kid, how broke are you now?"

She looked away stubbornly. "Oh, I've got enough to hold me for a while." But she went on with renewed vigor: "I want to see those crooks get put in jail. It doesn't seem to me as if the bank went under on account of the business depression, or any of those excuses."

"It didn't, baby. It went because those guys overstretched themselves. They made loans to their friends and to people who are important politically, without demanding the right kind of security. They made poor investments and spent too much of the money on schemes of their own. Then, when they had to pay off

some of their debts, they didn't have it. Somebody'll
go to the can. Don't let that worry you."

"Danny, it takes all the steam out of you. All the
money I saved— Tell me what happened, Danny.
There's this lawyer, what's his name?—Julius Moses—
wanting to organize the bank, and then somebody else
—God, how do they expect us to know what's going
on? I think they're all crooks!"

Dan laughed. "No, they're not. But they're using
the bank to make political trouble."

She flared: "So we're the goats for all your friends,
I suppose!"

"Don't get so excited. It's not my fault. It was like
this, and it's damned interesting—"

Her eyes widened. "Say, you're in on a lot of this
inside goings on. I bet you know all about the bank."

He shook his head. "I can figure a lot of the angles,
but I'm not in on it. What I mean is that my bosses
wanted to get Louis Wurstling out of the way."

"Don't make me believe they busted a bank to do
that!"

"Wait a minute, wait a minute, and I'll tell you.
You have to go back to November 10th or 11th.
Wurstling, who's one of the smartest lawyers there is,
was raising hell with the dope he was turning up in the
investigation. He's poison to the Hall on that account,
see? So they figured that if Wurstling could be made
a Special Assistant District Attorney, they at least

would be able to keep in touch with what his plans were. This way they don't know what's going to happen, and they get caught unawares."

The girl nodded, absorbed. He drank some more, lit a cigarette and leaned back. This was pleasant. He went on:

"So they made the official offer to Wurstling, but he saw through it and turned it down flat. Now get this. That happened before the bank closed, and right then nobody knew it was going to close. But the offer to Wurstling is interesting, and it has a connection because of what happened later.

"On the 2nd, the offer was made and rejected. On the 10th, the bank closed, and a depositors' committee was organized. Then Julius Moses was made attorney for the depositors' organization. That happened in one of two ways, as far as I can see it. Somebody very smart remembered that Louis Wurstling was a director of the Bank of the Empire State. The next step was to see if there wasn't some way of involving him in the bank investigation, and that way make trouble for him in his rôle of counsel for the Special Commissioner. Snappy reasoning, and they got the breaks. They knew that the cagiest lawyer they could put on the job was Julius Moses, not only because he's smart, but also because he and Wurstling have been bitter enemies for years. Moses was aching for a chance to get back at Wurstling for past defeats.

"What happened? Either Tully, in a roundabout way, suggested to Moses that he be depositors' attorney, or else Moses himself, seeing the chance, volunteered. I think that's what is really the truth, because Moses would want to protect himself too. Did you know that he drew sixty-five thousand dollars from one of the Empire State branches after three o'clock the day the bank failed? Well, that's why he was so damned anxious to be prosecuting attorney, instead of having to sit around and wait till somebody pinned that on him. This way he's got a chance to keep it quiet. Mix me another drink, sweetheart. This gassing makes me thirsty."

Betty got up and poured whisky and seltzer into his glass, handing it to him with a smile. "You're a sweet kid," he said.

"Keep your mind on the bank. You're going great."

"This is no fable in slang. Anyhow—one of those two ways Moses became attorney for the suckers. He goes to work examining records, questioning witnesses and all that, at various hearings. Then the boys, having allowed a decent interval to elapse, make Moses a Special District Attorney. There you are—Wurstling's enemies working together. A very neat stroke, but the papers saw the significance, and accused Quinn of getting in a backhand blow at Wurstling for having refused his own offer a month before. Quinn said, 'Oh, no, the appointment of Moses was not an attack on Wurstling.' Do you follow this, baby?"

She nodded, and laid her head against the back of the divan.

"Two weeks after that, Moses issued a subpœna for Wurstling as a witness—don't forget Wurstling was a Bank of the Empire State director—and Wurstling had to go on the stand. He made a good case, because he's just as shrewd as Moses. But Moses loved it, and all in all it looked bad for the heads of the bank. Then Moses, having dug up enough evidence to make even the bank-tellers look like highway robbers, turned the case over to the Grand Jury, Special Sessions. On the 11th of February—that's yesterday—they returned indictments against five of the bank heads, including Louis Wurstling, for felony and five other technical counts. Wurstling resigned as counsel for Martineau, and there you are. It took them a little over two months to nail Wurstling, but they nailed him. Now he's sick, and the trial will begin. It doesn't make much difference if they actually find Wurstling guilty. They got what they wanted, and Moses has his sixty-five grand and nobody says anything about it."

"But how about fixing the bank so we get our money back?"

"Oh, they will sooner or later, because the money seems to be there! The records are just a little screwy."

Silence held them both. Then Betty asked:

"That won't stop the investigations, will it?"

"Hell, no! Martineau is engaging other lawyers already. Good men, all right, though nowhere near so smart as Wurstling. The politicians can't stop the inquiry now. Too late."

Betty finished her first drink. Dan could feel in his pocket the bulk of his wallet containing another install-ment of his payments from Portis—his price, he told himself bitterly, for having turned stool pigeon in a large way. He said suddenly:

"Listen, kid, why don't you let me help you?"

She looked at him inquiringly, but shook her head. "I'm all right." Then she got up and went to the pan-try cupboard. "I'm hungry. How about a bite of food?"

"Sure."

He watched her while she made a collection of little sandwiches and started the coffee to perking. She was a good kid, he decided, and he wondered if she really had any money left at all. She wasn't working, and was banking on a contract she'd signed for a show due to open in the spring. She could starve to death mean-while, though.

Betty brought the tray full of food to the low taboret beside the divan. They ate.

He reopened the topic. "You let me help you. A loan,

if you like. I've got plenty and you don't have to worry about it, ever."

"Thanks, Dan. Forget it."

"No. Hell! We're pretty good friends, aren't we?"

She nodded, her mouth full of sandwich. He laughed and took the thousand dollars out of his pocket.

"Here. Tuck it in your bosom, and forget it. I don't need that dough."

"I'll take it, but I won't forget it."

"Now I feel better."

CHAPTER XVIII

The Lid Comes Off

IN THE month of February, Dan gave up going to
Colonel Portis' office. It had become too dangerous a
place for one who was working for the City Administration to risk being seen publicly. The old gent was
foaming at the mouth these days, and was openly triumphant at having, at last, given some weight to the
actions and opinions of the People's Franchise Union.
The press took it and him seriously now, and the office
on Wall Street was daily visited by reporters, photographers, interviewers and feature writers.

Colonel George Aristides Portis began to loom flam-
boyantly in the public eye as the man behind the steady,
piercing attacks on the reigning powers. Portis' latest
move had been an open-and-shut demand on Governor
Adams for the suspension and subsequent trial for
incompetence of Mayor Harding and District Attorney
Quinn. The demand was insistent, and was called "an
imperative move, if the Governor wishes to retain the
sympathies and support of his millions of friends."

Behold, Adams replied with an open manifesto:

"It is not for me at this time to accede to any hysteri-

cal requests for the exercise of extreme powers vested
in me by virtue of my office as Governor of the State.
Evidence is lacking. But if the situation is deemed sufficiently serious, the Constitution provides legal means—
an inquiry by the Legislature."

Dan had lost track of the maneuvers that caused
this. On February 19th, the Legislature voted on a
resolution brought forward by the Republican majority, and it was defeated by the votes of the Port-
chester representatives. These men were Republicans,
but the Hall must have bargained with them successfully to break their party allegiance and defeat the
inquiry. The Republican Party fell into an uproar over
the flagrant defection. Dan sensed something seriously
amiss.

There was subtle politics and shrewd thinking behind
Adams' attitude in appearing to advocate a move which
would antagonize the Hall, a large unit within the
State Democracy.

The speculation stayed in Dan's mind all that day,
and he kept his ears open for clews. He learned nothing
of interest during office hours, and he waited for the
evening.   There was scheduled a little party in the
Mayor's Chelsea Park home: Harding and Helen, Dan
and Betty, with Firenze and Lila. This would be the
first time in many months that Dan would face the
proprietress of the Mayor's Speakeasy. He had almost
forgotten what she looked like.

He picked up Betty for dinner and a couple of
drinks, and at nine they arrived at Chelsea Park. The
other four were there already, in the library, and Bozo
was kept busy bringing new glasses and set-ups. Harding greeted Dan:

"Hey, the demon lawyer! How're ya, boy?"

"Swell. Hello, Lila!"

She was casual. Firenze nodded and renewed his low-
toned conversation with Lila on a love seat by the
window.

Helen screamed: "Come on, folks, fill 'em up!
Helen's on the loose!"

Harding turned on the radio. Betty stood by him,
listening. Dan spoke to Helen: "What's new with you?
Working?"

She shrugged. "Oh, a couple of movie shorts! That's
about all. I'm resting." She looked it. Shadows under
her eyes, and her shoulders drooped. She finished a
drink quickly and mixed another. Firenze left Lila and
went out, presumably to telephone. Dan sat down by
Lila.

"Still in business, Lila?"

"Certainly. How're things with you?"

"Great. Haven't changed your mind, have you?"

She inspected him coldly: "No. Except I'm surer
than I was."

"Impossible." He watched her.

"Think so?" She accepted his lighter for a cigarette.

"There's only one double-crosser sitting on this seat."

He laughed: "You shouldn't reveal yourself so frankly. I might take you seriously."

She made an inarticulate sound of scorn. "You're too clever for yourself, Danny."

"Call me Danny-boy."

"If you're trying to irritate me, you're succeeding."

Firenze came into the room and joined them. Dan told her: "I'm glad to know it. How are you, Albert?"

"I'm very healthy."

Dan stared at him: "I'm glad to hear it, Albert."

Firenze's eyes were black dots. "We don't see you at the joint."

Lila threw in: "It isn't like the old days, Dan."

Dan stood up: "You're breaking my heart. Just for that I'll be in to see you. We can have a game of anagrams."

Nobody smiled and he went over to Betty. The radio was very noisy and he had to speak loudly: "Don't get drunk, will you?"

She shook her head. Her lips were smiling emptily. He looked at Harding and Helen doing a burlesque Apache dance around the room to the tune of "Just a Gigolo." The Mayor was light on his feet, as if he were dancing on eggs. Helen laughed.

Bozo reëntered with more drinks. Helen shrieked: "Say, babies, let's go up to Harlem later, whadda ya say?"

Lila agreed. "Only I have to stop in at the place later. That's my business."

Firenze said: "Let it ride one night, Lila. It goes all right. Everything's going smoothly."

Betty said to Dan: "I feel like Harlem tonight, Dan. How about you?"

"Great. Only don't get drunk. Maybe we'll have to move fast."

"I won't."

Harding cried: "One more round, ladies and gentlemen. Then we're off."

Helen said: "Make it three rounds, Billy. None of the joints get hot till much later. 'N' I wanta go where they do those dances. You know—" And she raised her skirt in front and did a couple of cooch steps. Harding grinned. Firenze bared his teeth.

Harding raised his glass in a toast: "Here's to us, sitting on the world!"

Everybody cheered. Bozo came in and said:

"Two gentlemen to see you."

"Who?"

"Mr. White and Mr. Tully."

Harding's face sobered, and he looked around quickly. "Show 'em in. And bring set-ups for 'em, Bozo."

A little silence fell and then Tully walked in, followed by White. Harding greeted: "H'lo, Tom. H'lo, Jim!" Everybody else sat tight, because White and

Tully were in no festive mood. Tully said straight at the Mayor:

"We'd like to talk to you. Can we get a little privacy?"

Harding fumbled: "Why—why, sure, I guess so, only—" He looked around at the girls. Dan got up. "Maybe the girls will go upstairs."

Helen squawked: "Aw, why can't we have a little party without—"

White told her sharply: "This is serious. You can help us by leaving us alone."

Lila stood up and walked slowly past White without looking at him. Dan gathered the Big Fellow knew who she was. His face reddened. This was the hostess of the speakeasy over which Harding had defied him—and he had to run into her at a party in the Mayor's home. Not so hot.

Dan patted Betty on the shoulder: "Toddle along with them, baby. See you later."

Tully said, as Dan started to walk out, not with the girls: "Dan, you stay here. You'll have to tell Quinn what happens."

Harding suddenly became conscious of the radio still blatting and turned it off. The quiet fairly sang. Firenze sat down again on the love seat. Dan stood leaning against a bookcase, and Jim White stood across the room from him. Tully sat down peaceably, content to let the Big Fellow do the talking.

White began: "First I'll apologize for breaking in this way. I don't have to tell you I have a good reason."

The Mayor blustered: "Why, glad to have you, Jim."

White ignored that, and went on: "Now I'm going to stop talking soft and speak right out. It seems I've got to treat you like children in diapers. That's what I'm doin' now." He lit a cigar calmly. Nobody said anything. Harding's mouth twitched.

"Now, I may not be the boss of you birds when it comes to straight city politics, but this has gone further than that. I hope it's clear to everybody, because otherwise I have no call to butt in on the Hall, even if I am a sachem. This is important in the whole State, and it may be more important than that, unless you all want the Hall to give the Democratic Party a black eye when the next Presidential election comes round. There was some cause for criticism a few years back, when Jimmy Walker was Mayor. But, gee!—this crowd is harder to handle than Walker and Curry!"

Harding protested. "I don't see what everybody's so excited about. Hell, somebody's always raising a stink and this doesn't look like anything different to me."

"You've got lots to learn. Trouble with you is you're so wrapped up in your own importance you can't see what's going on around you." White was talking louder. Dan could see his fingers itching to get around Harding's throat, as once they had been. "I've talked this out with Tom, and he's with me. I'm goin' ta talk turkey, and I want you to listen. Fitzhugh, you get this straight and give it to Quinn in the morning. I guess you're the only guy he listens to."

Dan grinned.

White continued, standing almost as if he were making a public speech. "I guess you think the city inquiry is definitely out, don't you?"

Harding: "Well, it was killed yesterday, all right, wasn't it? . . . Say, what's the idea of Adams turning against us? I don't like it."

Tully said sarcastically: "Think he cares?" Harding flushed.

"You wanta know that, eh?" White demanded. "I'll tell you. He refused to suspend you, as the People's Franchise Union asked, because nobody's given him a reason, publicly. But just because nobody has yet, don't think they won't go to work. I told Adams to do that, because in a matter of this kind, you fools can't seem to see that he's got to play along bigger lines. Why should he protect you against the people who might vote him in for President in a couple of years? You're only individuals, and he's thinking of the Organization. So'm I. If you can't understand that, you can't understand anything. Neither he nor I care a good God-damn about you, or anybody else, if it's going to hurt the Party. But it works both ways. We've got to put sense into your head, because you and your friends are doing your best to make fools of us all. I've committed myself for you in public, and I'll stick as long as possible. Get that straight. But in private I can tell you what I think. That's what I'm doing."

Harding pouted: "Well, don't get excited."

"Don't worry. Now, there's plenty of pressure, right in the State Democratic Party, for Adams to force an inquiry. They want to suspend you, then put you on trial. But he won't do that, for the simple reason it's too high-handed and unfair. But a legislative inquiry into the whole city won't hurt."

"Then he'll never get the Hall behind him again."

Tully said: "Don't be so sure. This thing is getting too big, and—"

"Well, what the hell's everybody jumping on me for? I'm not the only one!" Harding waved an arm.

White said: "I know. But you're the boss of your bunch of friends, and you're the Mayor. Listen to me some more. You think the inquiry bill was killed today. It was. You're right. But only because three Republican State Senators broke ranks and voted against the bill, because Dietrich got to them on a bargain basis. Well, I've been in Albany the last few days—I only left there this morning—and there's going to be hell to pay for those three birds. I'm here to tell you a guy came from Washington—Republican national headquarters, me lad—and gave them hell."

"So what?"

"So this: the bill will come up again, quick, and the Republicans will vote solid, and you'll have a city-wide inquiry to face. What do you think of that?"

The Mayor said: "All right. We'll make Adams veto it."

White sneered: "You'll make Adams do nothing. This whole affair is too big now. There's only one way to straighten this out, and by one means or another the public and the Republican and non-partisan groups will get it—and that's a thorough investigation. Every department of the city is goin' ta be looked into!"

There was a silence. Harding stared at the floor. Finally he said: "All right. We'll have it. We can get through all right."

Dan said: "If it's handled right, it'll be serious, but not disastrous."

White swung on him. "Thank God for one guy with sense. If it's handled right. That's the nub o' the whole thing. We gotta clear the decks for action. There's several people who've got control—and can give orders —that'll do it. Tom!"

Tully looked up surprised.

"I want you to cut the petty politics from now on, see?"

The thin-lipped mouth of the leader asked indignantly: "Talking to me?"

"Yes, I'm talkin' ta you! Start tomorrow. Tell these guys to shut up, stop squealin' like rats, and wait till

somebody with brains tells 'em what to say. Start with
yourself. Play close to the vest and use your brains.
Can the graft."

"Why, Jim——"

"Cut it out. I know there's plenty graft. Don't kid
me. Maybe you're not in on it, but you know all about
it. Stop it now."

Tully and White glared at each other. Tully lowered his eyes. "Okay."

White swung on Harding: "Now, that takes care of
the Hall. I told you to listen to me several months ago
and you thought you were too smart."

Harding flung at him bitterly: "Listen, my own life
is my own life. I can do what I God-damn please."

"You can like hell!"

"All right, suppose people start talking! That
doesn't belong in an official fight."

White laughed in his face. "Save that little speech
for the papers. Whether it belongs or not, it's going
to come out, and you can't help it. But you can protect yourself. I'll make you do it, by God!"

Harding sat down. His narrow shoulders drooped.
Dan felt a passing sympathy for him. Then he thought
of Helen upstairs.

White was thinking of her too. "Get this, Billy. If
somebody starts to make public talk about your own
affairs, you haven't got a leg to stand on. Your following comprises a large number of religious folk. Think

they like the idea of your wife floating around loose, and you having a girl friend? Think again. You've got to get rid of Helen Faire!"

Harding started. He stared at White, his face working. He said slowly, grinding out the words: "I'm good-natured, I guess, but I'm not going to let you or anybody else tell me what to do in my own personal—"

White pointed a finger at him: "You'll take orders, or overboard you go. How do you like that?"

Harding said: "You can't throw me over!"

"Without some real brains to tell you what to do, let me see you squirm out of it yourself."

Harding stared again. He was licked. He listened, as White went on: "We don't want any personal scandal mixing in—at least any more than we can help. How can you get rid of her?"

Firenze said: "Marry her to somebody."

Harding snarled at him: "Who the hell asked you?"

Firenze's eyes wandered, abashed. "Sorry, I thought it was a good idea."

"Best idea yet," said White. "That would stop any blackmail coming up. Letters and so forth. Who can you marry her off to?"

"She has a guy who's nuts about her," admitted Harding grudgingly. "Maybe that can be fixed. I think she'll like him."

Tully came in on White's side. "She must be made to like him."

"Come on. Figure it out now. You'll have to pay her plenty, of course; but you're not broke. You'll have to settle it tonight. Get goin'," White ordered.

Harding thought. Then he said: "This guy wants to go in the movie business."

White: "Is that what he wants most of all?"

Harding: "Yes."

"Can you get him a job? Quick?"

Harding nodded, throttling his own rage. "I can't fix it here, though. I'll have to go to California to see some friends of mine."

"Go ahead. Announce you're taking a vacation. Tomorrow."

"Hey, not so fast!"

"I said, announce it tomorrow. Tell her tonight, to fix the marriage end of it. Or you fix it yourself. See the guy in the morning. Give him dough, too, if you have to."

Harding compressed his lips. Then he bared his teeth. "The way it looks, I think I'll get myself a big movie job while I'm on the Coast."

White spoke slowly: "You're kidding, I guess, but just in case you get any ideas—you stick as Mayor of New York City until you're either whitewashed or removed!"

That was orders. Then, after a few seconds' silence, White added: "The rest is up to you. Come on, Tom."

He turned in the doorway. "Don't forget anything."
They were gone.

"I'm a son of a bitch!" said Harding. He picked up
a glass and smashed it on the floor.

Firenze urged: "I think you better do it."

His face red with fury, Harding went out in the
hall, and called up the stair-well: "Helen!"

"Coming!" Feet tripped on the steps. All three girls
came in. Dan said to Betty:

"You beat it along, kid. I have to stay."

Lila offered: "I'm going up to the place. Coming,
Albert?"

He shook his head. Helen demanded: "What's the
matter? The party over?"

Harding said: "Sit down, baby, I have to talk to
you. Albert, you have changed your mind. You go
with Lila. Dan, I want you here."

In three minutes, Harding, Helen and Dan were left
alone. The Mayor began:

"Listen, kid, I got a surprise for you. You're getting married."

She bounced out of her chair. "What? Like hell I
am!"

"Oh, yes, you are!" Harding looked away from her.
"Listen, we're all in a tough spot, and I want you to
go through a marriage with Dinny Keenan. Isn't that
the bird who's nuts about you? He'll jump at it."

She screamed: "Damn your nerve! I don't wanna marry that bum. Why should I? I'm doin' all right."

"You're not doing all right!" Harding snapped at her.

"Okay, then, I'm not! But to hell with you and your marriages. Why, I'd like to know?"

Harding explained with what little patience he had left: "You got to do it. Get this straight, for Christ's sake! There's going to be a lot of trouble for me in the next few months. The whole Administration is going to get raked over. And maybe the story of you and me will get out. If you're married to some guy, it can be denied successfully. See?"

She tossed her head. "All right, you're in trouble. That's your own fault. Why should I suffer?"

Harding pleaded: "Don't you want to help me, baby? Jesus, it'll be hell if all this comes out. You won't like it!"

A sudden inspiration lit up her glittering eyes. "You just want to get rid of me. This trouble racket is a stall. Well, if that's what it is—" she began to cry— "if that's what it is, you're treating me rotten!"

"Helen, for God's sake!"

She stamped a foot and screamed shrilly: "Cut it out, ya rat! You're stickin' a knife in me, that's what, and I won't stand for it!" She cackled, near hysterics: "Well, I hope it all comes out in the wash. You'll look silly, all right!" She laughed and laughed.

Harding: "For the love o' God, cut it out!" He looked helplessly at Dan. Suddenly, Helen ran out, screaming: "I won't do it! It's a dirty trick! I won't do it!"

Harding grabbed Dan's arm: "For Christ's sake, Dan, get hold of her. Make her do it. Offer her dough."

Dan hesitated a second, then ran downstairs after Helen. He swore when he banged an elbow against a corner. He seized his hat and coat from a chair and laid hold of Helen as she was struggling to get into her own coat.

"Lemme go!" she snarled.

Dan shook her. "Don't talk that way to me. Come on, I'll take you home!"

She looked at him, her face smeared with tears. "You're on his side, I guess. I'll go home alone."

He took her arm. She tried to break away. He slapped her hard across the mouth. She relaxed suddenly and got in a cab without saying anything. As they spun uptown toward her hotel, Dan remarked:

"I think you better do what Billy says."

"Marry Keenan? I will not. I don't care if it all comes out."

Dan soothed: "You're just sore now. That's all. If you think it over, you'll see it's the smart thing to do."

Her eyes gleamed in the dimness of the cab. "What's it to you?"

"I'm a friend of Billy's and a friend of yours. You better see that bird tomorrow and fix it. Billy will pay the expenses—anything within reason. You can get a divorce any time, you know, but this will help Billy a lot right now."

She was silent. "Suppose I don't?" she asked.

"Well, there's quite a few friends of Billy's that don't like you. They think you're unnecessary and in the way."

"What business is it of theirs if Billy and me're friends?"

Dan thought, and said: "Billy told you why. You take his advice and do it. Otherwise, you might get in a lot of very serious trouble."

The cab neared her hotel. She announced: "All right, I'll do it, but if anybody double-crosses me, I'll talk, and talk plenty."

"I wouldn't do that," he said.

She prepared to leave the cab. "You're the smart guy now, handing me mine. Well, get this, Mister, you're goin' ta get yours." She stepped out and went into her hotel.

Dan thought of Firenze, and wondered how much Helen knew about that situation.

CHAPTER XIX

The Finger Moves On

INSIDE of two weeks, they contrived Helen's marriage to Keenan—an obscure theatrical man. And the couple were on a honeymoon. Lots of publicity attended it, and lots of undercover whispering, the fringe of which crept into the daily papers. Coincidental with that, Martineau's inquiry forged on, nailing detectives, lawyers and magistrates. But the Hall had ceased largely to worry over that; it was beyond control. White's insistence on tactics that would not harm the very probable Presidential candidacy of Van Brunt Adams forced a policy that would reconcile Democratic safety with a last-minute escape for the city Organization.

The clearing of decks went on apace, in many departments. The Vice Squad was reorganized, not only to remove the offenders, but also to satisfy the outraged feelings of the vast majority of the Police Department against the few who had prospered illegally. Connie Dolan, the square Irish cop, tackled his job with silent tenacity and swept away many of the abuses that had flourished under the ridiculous Ollendorff.

But, like a vast current, the tide of opinion and demand was going against the administration. Little happened on the surface, but much beneath it. Dan went around with bated breath and sat on the edges of chairs, as did everybody else. As a result of Helen's perhaps random statement that he was going to get his, he worried spasmodically along personal lines and felt an increasing contempt for his big-scale stool pigeon activities. He wasn't backward in admitting, also, that a little deck-clearing for himself wouldn't hurt. In other words, if he could make a clean slate for Dan Fitzhugh now, he might save himself plenty trouble later on. A show-down was coming, and he didn't want to be caught between.

The night of March 5th, late, he called on Colonel Portis at his home. It was the first time he had entered the place—a duplex apartment on Fifth Avenue in the Eighties. He found the financier in a small but luxurious den. Dan sat down.

Portis said: "You are most certainly to be congratulated on your work, Mr. Fitzhugh. I am very, very pleased."

"Thanks."

"At first I didn't agree with you—in starting a fuse that would lead from the bottom to the top, but now I believe you had matters sized up accurately."

Dan hesitated. "Well, knowing what I did, that wasn't so much of a trick. It's still working."

"Hm! Yes. And we have also attained another goal—that of making the People's Franchise Union mean something."

"The papers do take it pretty seriously."

Portis smiled. "It is a great satisfaction to me to know that we now have some real power. We are in a position today to force the impeachment of Mayor Harding."

Dan pricked up his ears. "How?"

The old man chuckled. "We are drawing up a set of formal charges against the Mayor, which we shall file with Governor Adams. He will have to order a trial."

"Why?"

"Why? My dear boy, those charges are very serious!"

"Adams won't remove Harding just because you say so. I can assure you of that. Anybody in the know would say the same thing."

"But the Governor must act."

Dan shook his head. "A city-wide inquiry will be voted before the Legislature adjourns next month. It will include in its scope every phase of the city government. Adams knows that, and he won't risk a political misstep in advance."

The Colonel considered this. Then he said: "But the delinquencies of the Mayor are largely personal; he must be called to account!"

"The inquiry will come to him sooner or later. Then, if it gets too hot for him, he'll either resign, or at best, quit politics at the end of his term. Anyway, he's through. And here's another angle: Adams can't listen to self-appointed critics when the State is going to handle the whole thing."

"I take it, you would advise against these charges?"

"Not at all. They will keep public interest keyed up. That's what you want."

"Do you think that the charges against District Attorney Quinn, which are being prepared by another group of men like ourselves, will be disregarded also?"

"I'd say so; but maybe not. Quinn is smaller game— just a County official. Wait and see. But perhaps if ouster charges against Quinn are entertained, the same thing can be done to Harding later. It's hard to say." Dan paused. "There's something else I want to talk to you about. . . . I'm going to stop working for you."

Portis stared at him, surprised. "Stop? Why, we're just beginning! Aren't you satisfied with—?"

Dan said quickly: "Money's not the idea at all. I want you to let me out of our agreement. I figure I've given you most of the dope you needed, and the rest of the payment can slide. I'd rather not take it."

Portis regarded him studiously. "I don't understand this."

"Then I'll tell you frankly. I feel like a stool pigeon. And I want to stop feeling like one."

"That's absurd. You have performed valuable civic work."

Dan couldn't help smiling. "Maybe. But not the way I did it. Besides, I'm liable to get into a lot of trouble, and I don't want it to be any bigger than I can help."

Portis suggested: "If that's how you react, why don't you resign your political job and come with us openly? Then there will be no secret—nothing underhanded, as you seem to feel."

Dan stopped to think this over. Portis was being sincere and straightforward. He heard the Colonel say: "I'd hate to lose your services. You have been invaluable. You know that."

Certainly Dan knew it. Stool pigeons were invaluable, too. This whole business was giving him nerves. He replied: "I couldn't do that. They'd think there was something funny."

"But there's a fine political career ahead of you. You must leave the Hall sooner or later, or be dragged down with it."

Dan nodded. But he wasn't thinking of a career. He said: "Tell you what. I'll try and figure out some way of working with your crowd. I admire Martineau as a possible Party leader."

"Can't we come to a decision now?"

"Not unless you let me off the original bargain."

"I'd rather not."

They parted on that note.

The first thing Dan picked off his desk in the morning was an interoffice envelope marked to him, "Confidential." He tore it open and read:

"This is to inform you that your resignation from the post of Assistant District Attorney in charge of homicide cases is hereby requested.

"(Signed) Edward Quinn,

"District Attorney of New York County."

Dan sat down, cold. Fired. He couldn't think of a plausible reason, unless somebody had found out about Portis. He stuffed the memo in his pocket and visited the other private offices. After a check-up, he found that Blavitz, Ritchie and himself were the only Assistant D.A.'s, unless some subordinates had been included, who were being removed. Dan, Blavitz and Ritchie had all been held over on the staff from Jessup's régime. Nobody knew why they were being let out.

Dan went in to Quinn, who looked at him sorrowfully, and said apologetically before Dan could say anything: "I'm awfully sorry. I feel terribly about this."

"That's all right. I want to know why. This memo doesn't give a reason."

Quinn looked away. His lips worked nervously. "I—I really couldn't tell you why. You see, the order came from outside."

Dan stood still. "Tully?"

Quinn sneaked a look at him. Dan felt sorry for him. "No. The Mayor."

"Oh, I see! Well, that means Tully anyway."

The old ex-Judge sighed. "I suppose so. It's very distressing. And it hasn't all been explained to me."

Dan reminded him: "I told you all about White demanding a clearing of the decks for action."

"Yes, yes, I know. But why fire clever, valuable men?"

Dan walked to the door. "Thanks. I'm going down to see Harding."

He went over to City Hall, and sent his name in to the Mayor's office. In ten minutes, he was inside.

"Hello, Dan!" Harding greeted him cheerily. "Glad to see you before I go away."

"Going soon?"

"Two or three days." He stretched luxuriously. "I'm tickled to get out of this town for a while."

Dan said: "Well, I'm glad I caught you then. I want to know why Ritchie, Blavitz and myself are getting the air."

Harding shot a look at him. "Didn't Quinn tell you?"

"Said he didn't know."

Harding's face was serious, then broke in a smile. "Well, you don't have to take it seriously, Dan. We're just going ahead, getting things in running order."

"Then if I can count on you to take care of me, I don't have to worry."

"Sure, sure! That's it. See, we just want Quinn to have an out on the Carmody case if there's a blow-up over it."

Dan tensed. "What do you mean by that?"

"Well, don't you see, Dan?" Harding was staring out of the window, his fingers drumming on his chair arms. "He can say the Carmody case was mixed up by Jessup and his office."

"It was my idea, incidentally, for Quinn to make that talk during the campaign."

Harding smiled easily: "Yeah, I remember when you and he came down to see me. Well, that's the idea, see? It's not serious."

"What do I get in the way of a job?"

Harding's face lost its smile. "We-ell, I guess we can find something."

Dan pressed his jaws together. This was a different interview from what he had expected. Maybe this was just a way of easing him out, if he was right in thinking that Firenze was plotting to have him given the works. Then he'd better make a squawk. He began, holding himself in:

"I'm sorry, Billy, I don't quite get it. You're going to hang a rap on me for inefficiency, and I'm not going to get anything for it . . . Wait a minute, let me finish. I think it's a dirty trick. Let's go back a ways and see if I haven't got a few breaks coming to me. See if I haven't got good reason to burn up.

"You remember the nomination to the State Legislature I was supposed to get? What happened to it?

Walters objected and you walked out from under me."
Harding looked at the floor helplessly. "Didn't know
I knew that, did you? Then what did I get for pinching
the Rosenberg list for you guys? That job was worth
plenty, in one way or another, wasn't it? I got exactly
nothing except a pat on the back and some more promises. Now I'm through."

Harding put on an expression of impatience. "You
don't want to take that attitude, Dan."

"The hell I don't! I'm getting the works now, and I'm
good and sore. You can tell that to Tully or anybody
else. I've been the white-haired boy, and don't figure
you can—" He caught himself on the verge of anger.

"That's no way to talk to your friends, Dan. We'll
take care of you."

Dan stood up and stared down at the Mayor. His
muscles quivered with rage at the double-cross. He said:
"Maybe I'll feel better about it when I've had a chance
to think it over."

Harding smiled uneasily: "Yeah, that's it, Dan.
Drop in and see me when I get back from California,
and we'll talk it over some more. I'm busy and—"

"Sure, I know. Well, so long, Billy."

"So long, Dan. Glad to have seen you."

Outside he telephoned Miss Peabody: "Tell Colonel
Portis I have reconsidered and will continue to work
with him."

He went back to the office, shut the door and did some thinking. He was in a tough spot, and now he was going to get the Harding gang, if he went up in smoke at the same time. But that wasn't going to happen. Before he started to get them, however, he'd have to protect himself. Even though this removal was part of the deck-clearing plan, Firenze knew plenty and might have spilled it at the last to Billy Harding. Therefore, put Firenze out of the way. It was crazy to let Firenze live, in view of all that the wop had on Dan. The snitched copy of the Rosenberg list, and Firenze's hint that he knew Dan was doing business with Portis. Yes, and the personal spite growing out of the beating Dan had given him in Lila's presence, not to mention the affair of Louis the gun!

But it wouldn't be bad to start by finding out just how much Firenze knew. Lila was the key to that. For a long time now she had been the wop's exclusive sweetie, and he couldn't have failed to gab to her. Dan got her on the phone after lunch.

"Lila, this is Dan."

"Well?"

"I'd like to see you right before dinner, baby. I'm getting lonesome."

"You sound collegiate."

"All right. But are you going to be in?"

"Not to you. We're washed up."

"Listen, Lila. I want to see you. This is no business,

or anything. Purely a social visit. Let's have a talk, anyway. What can you lose?"

Silence. Then: "Okay. Six o'clock here."

He got there at a quarter of, and went up to her apartment. She was in a plain black-and-white dress, informal. He sat down.

"Surprised?"

She looked at him. "Not specially. What do you want?"

"That's no way to treat your old pal Dan. Come on, come to life. Welcome me back with open arms."

A smile tugged at her lips. "I ought to throw you out on your neck. I've got enough against you to make me hate you the rest of my life."

He said: "That's not my fault. Well, let's not argue about it." He was handling this with care. "I like you, and I missed you. So I came to see you again."

"I'm sorry. I don't believe you." She was walking around the room, moving ornaments, pulling up the shades, straightening chairs. She passed him; he seized her hand and pulled her down beside him on the divan.

"Come on, baby, be nice to me. We used to be good friends, didn't we? It isn't my fault you got sore at me."

"The hell it wasn't. You're a liar and a—"

He stopped her mouth with his hand. "We can straighten it out, can't we? We're not kids. Be a sport."

She put his hand away. "Sure, that's all right for

you to say, but how about—Dan, I wish I could hate you." Her gaze grew a trifle softer.

He worked fast. "Listen, let's go for a ride. I'll get the car and we can have a good long talk."

"I'm suspicious of you."

He stood up, offering his hand. "All right, be suspicious. But can't I come to see you because I like you?"

She sighed and went to put on her coat. They taxied to his garage, got the coupé and started up toward Riverside Drive. He said:

"You don't know how glad I am to see you."

"I'll swear you want something. You never talked like this before."

He went slower through traffic. "I never went so long without seeing you. Hell, can't you believe I like you?"

"Naturally. But you'd throw that over if you could help yourself."

He reached over and patted her hand. "Suppose you save that talk for later. Let's be sociable now, enjoy the air. Let's have dinner in Tarrytown."

"I have to be back at the club by eleven."

"That's easy. It's nearly seven now. We'll be there in an hour. Back by eleven easily." He speeded up again on the Drive.

She was silent for a long time. Then she leaned slightly against him. He didn't move. She said softly: "You know, I am glad to see you, Danny-boy."

"That's more like it."

"You know—I like Albert—but somehow or other, Italians—"

"I know. Never know what the hell they're going to do."

She sighed restfully. "I wish we hadn't had that fight, Dan. You and me."

"Well—" He started to say something about the wop, but changed his mind: "We can forget it now, baby."

More silence. Then: "Just let's not talk about Albert and all the political mess. It's getting me scared."

"Okay with me. Did I tell you I got fired today?"

She sat up straight and looked at him with concern. It struck him suddenly that she really was terribly fond of him. He felt that he could return the feeling. She said: "Oh, Dan! Why?"

"Don't know yet. Well, let's not talk about it. Just you sit beside me—there—and—"

"This is swell, Dan."

"Sure it is, baby."

After dinner in Tarrytown they talked for a long time, nothing special, but just conversation, getting acquainted again, used to each other. Dan and she thoroughly enjoyed themselves. At eleven they started back, when Lila said:

"I wish I never had to go back to that damned speakeasy."

He thought for a moment. "We don't have to go back tonight."

She was still. He added: "Some friends of mine run

a quiet place up behind Spuyten Duyvil." That was Jack's crowd. Dan frequently used it for a hideaway.

She said quietly: "Dan, I—I better not."

He knew she was thinking of Firenze. He answered: "What the hell? Call up and say you're with friends. Some stall."

She said with finality: "All right. Stop at the next place where I can telephone."

Dan had expected to feel triumphant. But he didn't. He felt a certain pleasure. He drove to the roadhouse on the hill above Spuyten Duyvil. Jack, whom he had last seen in the Tenth Avenue speakeasy, greeted him, looking sideways at Lila. The roadhouse had a front room with a few tables, equipped to serve meals to tourists. There was a small reading room, and upstairs several large, airy rooms for guests. Jack showed them to a pair of rooms connecting and sent up something to drink. Later several cars drove up, and people came inside. The roadhouse was used by Jack's organization for liquor storing and social headquarters.

It was Friday night and they had the week-end ahead of them. Lila dropped her hostility, and it seemed to Dan like the old days. They had a highball and went to bed.

In the morning Dan had to go to the office. He left Lila with the promise he'd be back by two o'clock, and drove in. It was ten by the time he arrived. He cleared up his desk, beginning to take out his personal stuff preparatory to leaving in two weeks. At a quarter to eleven one of his assistants came in:

"Murder case 'way uptown. I'm going out on it."

"Okay. Phone me later when you find out what it is."

Five minutes later, his phone rang.

"Hey, Dan, this is Jack." The gangster's tight-lipped voice was husky with excitement.

"Yeah."

"Say, the joint was shot up this mornin'. I just got away. George and Sammy got hurt."

"What else?"

"Your dame got bumped."

Dan's knuckles went white as he gripped the phone. "Tell me what else. Who did it?"

"I recognized a couple o' the guys. They drove up in two cars and barged right in. Had their nerve with 'em, all right. They started shootin' right away, and we beat it. What the hell? I think I nailed one o' the bums. A bunch o' wops from downtown. The same gang that got Louis, ya know?"

"Sure I know. Where're you?"

The voice chuckled. "I'm gettin' some guns together. We'll nail those guys in a coupla days. Meanwhile they's nobody left in the joint up there except the gal. They put four bullets in her."

"Was what's his name there?"

"Ya mean Firenze? Yeah, he plugged her himself.

Boy, he musta thought you was there, the way he come in!"

"All right, Jack. I'll see you later."

This was the case, he guessed, his assistant had gone on. He was down in his car right away and soon sped uptown. He thought fast as he went.

Firenze, returning to the Club, must have learned that Lila had left with him. Then, by enlisting his gangster friends in combing over all of Dan's known haunts, he had found the Spuyten Duyvil inn toward morning. He could picture the wop mustering his forces and going to the attack. Only Dan had not been there, which Firenze may or may not have known. It was a possibility that Dan had had the good luck to slip out while they were preparing for the rush.

But why, if Dan wasn't there, go to the trouble of putting Lila away? Still that was clear enough, if Firenze was as smart as Dan thought. The garlic-grower must have reasoned that Dan had gone back to Lila with the intention of pumping her for all she knew. There was no other logical reason; for Firenze would never believe, even had it been the truth, that Dan was really gone on Lila. Firenze couldn't bank on the fact that Dan had not learned anything, and like a true son of the Mafia he was taking no chances. That she must have known plenty was now obvious.

Dan tore up the hill road to the inn and jumped out. Already parked there was a large sedan belonging to

City Hall—Firenze must have come back in that. A Police car and two touring cars stood by. Dan entered the building. Several patrolmen stood around, waiting. Dan went upstairs to the rooms he and Lila had occupied the night before. There was sweat on his forehead. The Medical Examiner, two Homicide Squad men, his own assistant from the D.A.'s office, a photographer and two male stenographers—the regular bunch were there.

Plus Firenze. Dan looked at Lila. They had nailed her before she had had a chance to get up out of bed. Bullets had plowed through her torso and head and neck from several angles. Dan figured they didn't know he wasn't there and had riddled the place, to be sure to get one or both. Firenze had shot Lila himself, Jack had said; but there had been a regular fusillade from other guns.

The bed was a mess of dark, stagnant red blood and chalky skin. Lila's face was buried in a pillow, and the hands clenched on a blanket. Dan thought of Maria Blake.

He heard Firenze say: "Too bad. She was a good friend of mine. Ran a high-class speak in Fifty-second." For the benefit of the cops and stenographers, he added: "You knew her, too, didn't you, Mr. Fitzhugh?"

Dan looked across the bed straight into his eyes. "Yes. I knew her, too."

Then they took pictures of Lila.

CHAPTER XX

The Wrong Man Gets Killed

A FEW nights after that, Dan found his hotel room turned off: the contents of the bureau drawers scattered around, the closet emptied on the floor, and his desk rifled. But nothing was gone. Dan straightened out the confusion, and did not squawk to anybody. He moved to a higher floor in the hotel the next day.

Two nights later, as he was walking to his hotel from the garage—it was about three A.M.—a pair of bullets whanged past him into a wall. He ducked into the shadows and watched a touring car turn the corner. From then on, he stuck to lighted streets and tried to be indoors at an early hour.

The afternoon of April 11th, he went down to the District Attorney's office. Two weeks before, he had turned over his work to a new man, and had moved out after six years in the same spot. He felt lost, but full of plans. He walked in to talk to Quinn.

He found the old man in a nervous, upset state. Ouster charges had been filed against him and hearings were scheduled to begin soon before Martineau. Steinmetz, prominent lawyer and friend of Harding's, was to defend him.

Dan said: "Sorry to hear what's happening. Do you think it's serious?"

The Judge answered: "Oh, I don't know, Dan! I wish I had you and the other boys with me. Somehow, all these new faces—you know—and all this coming on top of it! Sit down, Dan, and have a cigar."

"Thanks. I think Steinmetz ought to be able to get you out."

"It isn't that so much. It's just that there's been a lot that's hard on my nerves. I'm afraid I paid too much attention to what Tully was saying, and neglected this office."

"Oh, no!" Dan was sorry for the poor man, harassed by worries and about to face disgrace. In his heart, he knew that they'd get the old man. It was all right to blame it on his assistants, and on the Federal Attorney's office, and the Banking Department, and the Prohibition Unit, and all that; but in the final analysis, a public prosecutor was either energetic or he wasn't. It came down to that. Ex-Judge Edward Quinn was some twenty years too old to be energetic. He added: "What're they going to do for you?"

The gray eyes shifted distractedly. "Oh, what can they do? Have a conference, talk, talk, talk about the Hall, about the Party, about—I tell you, Dan, that's small consolation for having a career smashed!" He almost wept.

Dan kept silent. Quinn added, in a burst of anguish: "I didn't want to be District Attorney. They forced it on me as a reward." He had the courage to emit a bitter laugh.

"Well, maybe they can help you now. Are they going right to work? They ought to." He was looking for a lead.

Quinn nodded: "Tonight there's another conference being called at Tully's. Just a few of us—you know—White and Tom and Harding. Dietrich and Calloway, too, I suppose."

"Sure," said Dan. "The usual thing."

Quinn sat up. His old gray eyes gleamed with his last hope. "Yes, but I understand tonight's the biggest ever. Of course, you won't mention this to a soul. But White's got some sort of record that's part of his talk. It sounds rather wild and improbable, I think."

"Record? Probably just a summing up of everything that's happened."

"No, it's more than that, Dan. I don't know why I'm telling you this, but I've got to talk to somebody who'll listen." He was pathetic. "Tom just dropped a few words to me, and I gather White has got hold of some letters written by Crandall—you know, Police Commissioner before Ollendorff—telling all about how the Administration made him mishandle the Rosenberg case."

Dan smoked with conscious care. "Where in hell would he get a thing like that? That's dynamite."

Quinn sighed. "It all seems very unimportant to me."

"But letters telling all that! Letters to whom?"

"God knows. His wife, or sister, or somebody. Anyway, the idea is that White is going to lay all Mr. Harding's record on the table, and a definite plan of campaign will be mapped out. I suppose they'll decide about me, too."

"Better work fast. The City-wide inquiry was voted yesterday, and Martineau will get right to work."

"I know. Harding is framing his reply to the People's Franchise Union, and—"

"You know as well as I do that Adams won't listen to those charges. Not with a legislative inquiry coming along. He can't."

Quinn moved his hands restlessly. "I wish they had voted the inquiry before my proceedings were started."

"You're better off this way." Dan said it to comfort him, but he knew the old man was through. He wondered about those Crandall letters. It sounded fantastic. He remarked:

"White will have plenty to say tonight."

Quinn stared out of the window, without answering. His gray cheeks sagged. Dan got up.

"Well, I wish you lots of luck, Judge. It was a pleasure to work with you."

The doomed veteran smiled gratefully. "Thanks,

Dan. I wish you were with me now. I guess it won't be very long before I—"

Dan cut in: "Don't worry about it. Incidentally, I won't mention, ever, that you told me—"

"Oh, no! I'm sure you won't."

They shook hands.

Dan went back to his hotel. He changed his clothes and did a lot of heavy thinking. This was his chance. Firenze was sniping at him, and he had to get the whole lot of them. They had played him enough dirty tricks. When he thought of how Billy Harding had ditched him, he boiled. If only he could lay hands on the Crandall letters.

In his time, he had heard a pack of wild stories to the effect that the ex-lawyer and crony of the Mayor had left a written record of how the Administration had forced him to mishandle the Police Department. The gossip came back quite clearly now to Dan's mind. What more likely than that Crandall had included in his "confession" the facts about how they had instructed him to let the Rosenberg murderer go? And it was a pretty well accepted fact that on his sudden and ruthless removal from the Commissionership, Crandall had died, literally, of a broken heart; defeated and crushed. In the circumstances, it was probable that he had poured out his woes on paper, though how White or anybody else had managed to get hold of the documents was difficult to see.

Dan felt a stab of real sympathy for Quinn, who was just another goat to be thrown to the wolves. From the D.A.'s words, it was clear that Jim White was still learning things about the inner workings of the City, and that he was going to lay down the law once again to Harding. The Big Fellow's indictment of the play-boy Mayor would be a scorcher this time. But Dan doubted, from all he had heard and seen, that Harding knew of the Crandall papers.

Dan saw that he had the chance of his life that night to make the impeachment of the Mayor a certainty. Somehow, he must get into Tully's house, hear what was said, and if possible steal the Crandall letters. It sounded difficult, but Dan was thoroughly familiar with Tully's house. There were three entrances besides the front, and the servants would probably be sent out for the evening. The Tully family would go to the movies. Dan knew of the music room next to the library, where the conferences were always held. It was possible to reach that by coming up the servants' stairway. To hear all that was said would be comparatively easy. It would then be up to him to create his chance to pinch the letters. Once that evidence was in Portis' hands, a single blast would knock the whole city into the next century.

At six o'clock, after napping for an hour, Dan went out to eat. He had vegetable soup, a minute steak with potatoes, a piece of chocolate layer cake and two cups of coffee. He smoked and had another cup of coffee, waiting for darkness. He figured that the conference of the master minds would hardly begin until eight or a little after.

Then he started for Tully's house downtown. He took the subway to the most convenient station, got out and walked west. He turned into the street on which Tully's house stood at an angle from the main avenue. It was a street of small residences, tea rooms and remodeled walk-ups. At that second, it was deserted. Two men mooched toward him on the opposite sidewalk, before he realized they were there. He walked faster.

He looked behind. A man was following him. A woman came out of a basement, passed him and went her way. The street was empty of vehicles. Then a car headed into it. Dan started to run. Firenze was sniping at him again. He had his own gun out. The car ground by, and a sub-machine gun spat through the curtains. Dan lost his hat. He heard a woman scream. Somebody shouted.

The men on the other side of the street ran toward him. Dan didn't look back. He had more than a hundred yards to go to the corner. He thought how silly they were to want to kill him when the root of the trouble was Mayor William T. Harding. Dan laughed. He was getting near the corner.

He heard the car again, coming the other way. Everything seemed to happen very slowly. He wondered why the shooting didn't bring the cops. Then he heard a police whistle. The sub-machine gun spat again, and something hit him in the back and made him stagger.

That made him mad. One of the two men chasing him he saw was Firenze. He fired at the wop, and saw him drop his gun and hold his shoulder. Then Firenze shouted something.

Dan's back felt very warm, and his stomach hurt him suddenly. He wondered if the chocolate layer cake was giving him trouble. He fired twice more. Sweat ran in his eyes. Nobody came. Hell, you couldn't have fireworks like this—and nobody come! He shot with precision, and saw one man sit down on the sidewalk and lie over slowly.

Dan turned around, with the idea of running in a new direction. But the buildings stood still. The pavement stood still. He looked down and saw his feet weren't moving.

"I'll be God-damned!" he mumbled.

Somebody said loudly: "The bastard!"

He thought how hot it was for April. His stomach hurt him with a fresh, sharp pang. Lousy cake—never eat in that place again! Abruptly, the street lights went out. All the lights went out. Dan fell on his face.

THE END